"Come out, come out, wherever you are!" Ada called into the well, raising a muffled echo and a distant giggle from the depths. She fumbled a penny out of her purse and dropped it, waiting for the plunk. *"I wish," she began, bending over the invisible water.*

The penny hurtled back up the well and past her face. Ada pressed herself against the tree, staring at the ring of limestone.

"A-a-ada!" called Matilda.

Impulsively Ada leaned over the well again and dropped in her peloncillo *candy. "I wish"—she gabbled the first thing that came into her head—"I wish I lived a hundred years from now!"*

Plunk! *said the water, far below.*

And there was a roaring in her ears.

***

Amber snatched an atomic fireball out of her purse, popped it out of its wrapping, and leaned over the well, so far that gravity tugged at her high-riding hair ribbon. "I wish," she gabbled, dropping the round cinnamon candy, "I wish I lived a hundred years ago!"

Plunk! *said the water, far below.*

And the world fell silent.

"Highly original, and a true page-turner".—*Publishers Weekly*

Also by Peni R. Griffin

Otto from Otherwhere
A Dig in Time
Hobkin
The Treasure Bird

SWITCHING WELL
Peni R. Griffin

PUFFIN BOOKS

Hi, Mom. You Finally Get One.

PUFFIN BOOKS
Published by the Penguin Group
Penguin Books USA Inc., 375 Hudson Street, New York, New York 10014, U.S.A.
Penguin Books Ltd, 27 Wrights Lane, London W8 5TZ, England
Penguin Books Australia Ltd, Ringwood, Victoria, Australia
Penguin Books Canada Ltd, 10 Alcorn Avenue, Toronto, Ontario, Canada M4V 3B2
Penguin Books (N.Z.) Ltd, 182-190 Wairau Road, Auckland 10, New Zealand

Penguin Books Ltd, Registered Offices: Harmondsworth, Middlesex, England

First published in the United States of America by Margaret K. McElderry Books,
an imprint of Macmillan Publishing Company, 1993
Published in Puffin Books, 1994

1 3 5 7 9 10 8 6 4 2

LIBRARY OF CONGRESS CATALOGING-IN-PUBLICATION DATA
Griffin, Peni R.
Switching well / Peni R. Griffin. p. cm.
Summary: Two twelve-year-old girls in San Antonio, Texas,
Ada in 1891 and Amber in 1991, switch places
through a magic well and try desperately to return to their own times.
ISBN 0-14-036910-4
[1. Time travel—Fiction. 2. San Antonio (Tex.)—Fiction.] I. Title.
PZ7.G88136Sw 1994 [Fic]—dc20 94-15025 CIP AC

Printed in the United States of America

Contents

CHAPTER ONE

April 24, 1891

Odett, of course, had spent her weekly nickel, and wanted Ada to share hers when they passed El Dulcero, the candy man, on their way home. A bevy of schoolchildren were already crunching pecan-filled *envueltos* and chewing flat, nutty *pipitorios*. "Eight years old is big enough to manage money," Ada began, putting her almost-thirteen years of authority into her voice.

"It's no good asking that skinflint," said Billy Streicher, waving a red *melcocha* stick as long as his forearm. "You know she pinches her pennies so tight she chokes the Indian to death!" He inserted an end of candy into a corner of his insufferable smile.

Ada stuck her nose into the air. "I don't have any mind to spoil my little sister like some folks I know spoil theirs."

"Why not?" asked Billy, with his mouth full. "Girls can't manage money. So why make her suffer?"

"Women are better managers than men, any day," retorted Ada.

"I don't see where it's your business, so there!" piped up Odett loyally.

"As I was going to say when I was so rudely interrupted," Ada said, turning her back on Billy, "you're big enough to know better, but since it is a special day, we'll get some candy. Just don't take it for a precedent."

"What's the president got to do with anything?" asked Odett.

Billy laughed. "Not *president*, *pre-ce-dent*. She means don't expect her to do it again."

Ada ignored him and frugally bought four *peloncillos* at two for a nickel. Odett squealed with delight. "Two apiece!"

"Don't be a little goose," said Ada, trying to juggle three *peloncillos* and her books. "The extras are for Toby and Doris."

"Here," said Billy. "I'll carry your books."

"No, thank you," said Ada, fitting them under her left arm, two candies in her left hand, and one in her right.

"Hold up, we'll walk with you." Billy popped his *melcocha* out of his mouth, popped two fingers in, and whistled. Pinkie, Dot, and little Sallie came variously walking, skipping, and trotting, all carrying different colors of *melcocha*. Pinkie was the only one who did not look happy to be whistled for. "What is it?" she demanded. "Viny was showing me her new jacks."

"It's time to get home," said Billy. "You know how Mary Reba'll take on if we're late to lunch again." The way Billy swaggered along the board sidewalk in the midst of this gaggle of sisters, as if he owned them all, set Ada's teeth on edge.

"Huh! I don't know what you think she'll do to us!" Pinkie tossed her head, to the peril of her hat.

"Mamma said the next time we made Mary Reba threaten to quit, she'd make us sorry," said Dot, her skirts flipping against her white-stockinged knees as she skipped ahead.

"She'll make you miss the parade," said Odett.

"Oh, no!" cried Sallie, who was only six.

"Don't worry," said Billy, holding her hand as they crossed the street on the brick walkway. "I'll see you get to the parade—if there is one."

"Why shouldn't there be?" Odett tilted her head back to examine the white clouds overhead. "It won't rain again. I don't think." She sounded anxious. The parade—originally planned as part of the ceremonies for President Benjamin Harrison's visit last week—had already been rained out once, and the streets were still muddy.

Billy shook his head, biting the end of his *melcocha* and saying, around it: "Those ladies running it don't know what they're about. Why, I bet no two of them agree on where they're supposed to get the buggies together." He looked at Ada and grinned.

Ada, still smarting from the way her teacher, Old Maid Grundage, had graded her essay "A Woman's Sphere," wanted to smack him. "Bunkum," she snapped. "Women are better organizers than men!"

"Our pappa says, if the parade committee is an example of how ladies run things, it's a good thing they can't vote."

"If women could vote, we'd be a lot better off!"

Odett, spotting her own pappa, dashed ahead before Billy could reply, her boots resounding on the sidewalk.

Glad to end the conversation with the last word, Ada followed.

Pappa waited, his gray mustache bristling and his gray suit with the striped trousers almost as neat as when he left the house that morning. "Slow down and walk like ladies! What is that you have?"

"*Peloncillo*, Pappa!" Odett flourished her half-eaten cone of brown sugar. "Ada bought some for Toby and Doris, too."

"Ah," said Pappa. He relieved Ada of her books—just as well, since her elbow was beginning to ache—and they walked toward the corner where the yellow-brick businesses and open lots gave way to well-spaced houses and china trees. Odett chattered about getting the afternoon for a holiday. Pappa frowned.

"This parade does not even begin until five o'clock," he said. "Why should children not be in school?"

"Oh, but some of the children are in the parade!" exclaimed Odett. "And they have to get dressed up, and help with the flowers."

Ada concentrated on keeping the flies off her *peloncillo*. The noon heat was like a hand pressing atop her head. Delicious dinner smells wafted out into the street; but at dinner, she would have to tell Mamma and Pappa about her essay.

The Streichers bade them good-bye at the corner, trooping up to their limestone house. Proceeding toward the tin roof and white walls of their own home, the Bauers passed the Haunted Lot, where scrubby, yellow-flowered huisache shrubs crowded under a huge live oak. Doris and Toby came tumbling into the street to meet them. Doris, who was five, was reasonably clean except for a smudge

4

down her front; but three-year-old Toby's white skirts were filthy. Pappa scooped both of them up regardless as they jabbered at him.

"Doggy!" crowed Toby. "I want doggy!"

"There wasn't a dog!" Doris glared at Toby. "You went on the Haunted Lot! The ghost'll get you!"

"Hush," said Pappa. "You know there're no ghosts. And Toby, you know you can't go in the lot. You might fall in the well and then we wouldn't have our Toby anymore."

"Was too a dog," grumbled Toby.

Ada groaned, knowing who would have to clean up Toby. "You two are more bother than you're worth," she said. "Why did I bother to buy *peloncillo* for children who can't behave?"

"*Peloncillo!*" screamed Doris. Pappa hushed her.

By the time Ada got the little ones clean, everyone else— even Matilda and Simpson, home from the high school— was seated around the dining room table, ready to say grace.

Mamma smiled as Ada put Toby into his high chair, but she looked tired. Pappa led grace; then Odett started chattering about the parade. Frieda, the hired "girl," dished up the soup before sitting down. Her face was damp from the heat, and sagging. Ada tried to get Toby to eat his food instead of playing with it.

At last Mamma turned to Ada. "What about that essay? Did you get it back today?"

"Yes, ma'am," said Ada, not looking at her. "Miss Grundage said if the spelling and punctuation hadn't been perfect, she'd have been tempted to fail me."

Pappa, down at the other end of the table, couldn't

5

possibly have heard; but Simpson did. "Failed you? Pshaw!"

"Tempted to fail me," mumbled Ada. "She didn't do it."

"What did she think was wrong with it, I'd like to know?" demanded Mamma.

Ada shrugged; but Pappa was looking at her. "Miss Grundage disagreed with me, that's all."

"To what did she object?" asked Pappa.

"Well—the topic was 'A Woman's Sphere.' " She focused on Mamma's approving face. "I said the earth was woman's sphere and when we got the vote we would . . . would show what we could do."

Pappa cleared his throat. "I gather, Mrs. Bauer, that you had read this composition."

"I did," said Mamma, facing him down the table. "It was a very well-reasoned piece."

"Since she doubtless borrowed your reasons, it is not surprising that you thought so," said Pappa. "What did Miss Grundage say, Ada?"

Ada grew hot to the roots of her hair. "She said no true woman wanted to infringe on a man's privileges and desert the sacred calling of the home."

"Hmph," snorted Mamma. "She might as well say the only reason she's teaching is because she can't catch a man."

"She shouldn't assign controversial topics if she's going to penalize students for their views," said Matilda.

"Why should a woman's sphere be controversial?" Pappa tore off a hunk of bread. "Miss Grundage should not threaten to fail students for their opinions, but where is the gain in women expanding into politics, if it means the home is neglected? Just today, Toby and Doris ran wild in the empty lot—"

"I did not!" objected Doris, but his stern look quelled her.

"Did anyone here even know they were outside? Toby might have fallen to his death in that old well."

"I keep saying we need another girl to help," said Mamma. "Frieda's husband . . . came visiting"— (So that was why Mamma and Frieda both looked frazzled! Ada was glad not to have been home when he came. Frieda's husband scared her with his wild-eyed shouting and fist waving.)—"and I was washing windows. An orphan from—"

"If Matilda were not learning to make useless messes in chemistry tubes, we would not need someone else's orphans to look after our children," interrupted Pappa.

"They're not useless, Pappa," said Matilda.

Ada ate her soup as the argument raged about her head. She should have written an essay Miss Grundage would have liked—but that would have been next door to lying.

Soon Mamma, Pappa, and Matilda were arguing whether Matilda should stay home this afternoon, or fulfill a promise to a friend and help decorate a buggy. "Ada can look after the little ones," said Mamma. "Can't you, Ada?"

"Yes, ma'am," said Ada. "May I be excused, please?"

Permission obtained, she carried her dishes to the kitchen, snatched up her half-sucked *peloncillo*, and escaped out the back door. Unhesitatingly, she ducked into the Haunted Lot.

The well was in the middle of the lot, under the live

7

oak. It was only a limestone-walled hole in the ground, and the tree roots had grown around it like embracing arms. Ada sprawled on the roots, feeling the trunk strong and rough against her back, and sucked *peloncillo*. The brown paper had torn, so she took out her handkerchief as an extra layer of protection against stickiness. A mockingbird sang, yellow leaves fluttered down, and the well smelled of moss.

It wasn't fair. Simpson was free this afternoon, but nobody thought of making him watch the children.

Nothing was fair. Her essay had only told the truth. Mamma talked all the time about how women were trapped by the demands of large families, fashions that crippled their bodies, laws that crippled their wills. All that would change when women got the vote. There'd be no men like Frieda's husband, spending all her money and earning none himself. There'd be dress reform, she thought, loosening her sash, and professionals to look after small children instead of big sisters. Old maids like Miss Grundage wouldn't be teachers. Ada sucked *peloncillo* happily.

Somebody giggled.

Ada sat up straight. "Who's there?"

The giggle was behind the tree, but when she looked, she saw only a squirrel streaking up the trunk. She heard a small splash and, when she turned again, saw two wet footprints no longer than the tip of her index finger smudging the limestone.

The mockingbird stopped singing.

Ada had read her *Alice in Wonderland*, and the faily tales in *St. Nicholas* magazine. I'm dreaming, she thought; but the sticky paper in her fist did not feel like a dream. Something marvelous will happen, she thought; but the world was still.

"Come out, come out, wherever you are!" she called into the well, raising a muffled echo and a distant giggle from the depths. She fumbled a penny out of her purse and dropped it, waiting for the *plunk*. "I wish," she began, bending over the invisible water.

The penny hurtled back up out of the well and past her face. Ada pressed herself against the tree, staring at the ring of limestone.

"A-a-ada!" called Matilda.

Impulsively Ada leaned over the well again and dropped in her *peloncillo*. "I wish"—she gabbled the first thing that came into her head—"I wish I lived a hundred years from now!"

Plunk! said the water, far below.

And there was a roaring in her ears.

CHAPTER TWO
April 26, 1991

Amber's mother parked on the street, since the Streicher Children's Center lot was full. The air, too heavy to breathe, smelled of smoke. What a waste of a good house, Amber thought as they walked through the playground to the tall, red-roofed limestone building. The Center had been a single-family home once, but now it housed runaways and children whose parents couldn't take care of them. None of them appreciated the elegant bay windows and fireplaces and molded ceilings. None of them appreciated her mother, either. When Amber was a billionaire, she'd build a new center, move the children into it, move this house out to the country somewhere, and live in it.

When they entered the cool, tidy hall, someone was screaming upstairs, and Dr. Cunningham was coming down, looking frazzled. "I'm glad you're here, Grace," she said. "Go explain to that Gonzales kid why he can't go to the parade."

"Why can't he?" asked Mom. "And what are you doing here?"

"I couldn't find anybody whose job it was to deliver the evaluations, so I stopped by." Dr. Cunningham dropped into a chair. "Carla hadn't been talking to me five minutes when a fight broke out. We broke it up, but the Gonzales kid mouthed off at Carla, and she grounded him, so now he's screaming. See what you can do with him, will you? He'll listen to you."

Mom made an exasperated noise and headed upstairs, her tennis shoes thumping on the carpet. Amber swung on the newel post. Why couldn't Mom have a normal job—or even do without a job at all? Dad made enough money without the little bit Mom's social working brought in. He said so all the time.

Dr. Cunningham took a pill out of her purse, swallowed it, and snapped her purse shut. "So. How've you been doing, Amber?"

"Okay," said Amber, swinging on the newel post— hands locked around its knob, purse dangling from her wrist, one foot braced against the stair, one foot swinging free and heavy, sundress and tied-back hair swishing pleasantly.

"Good," said Dr. Cunningham. "A lot of kids would be really upset. And it's normal, of course; but it does no good."

Swing, swish. "Upset about what?"

"Oh, everything—the separation, the—" She stopped talking as Amber stopped swinging.

"What separation?" asked Amber.

"Oh, dear," said Dr. Cunningham. "Naturally, I figured if it was already on the grapevine—look, you should ask your mom." She rubbed her forehead. "I've got a splitting headache. Maybe I'll skip the parade."

Amber's weight stretched her hands as they clung to the newel post. "Somebody told you Mom and Dad were splitting up?"

Dr. Cunningham stood. "I heard it around. I've got to go."

She hurried out as Amber lowered herself to the floor. The screaming had stopped. Mom would be down soon, leading a herd of children. They would all troop under the highway to Alamo Plaza, to watch the Battle of Flowers parade. They would eat cotton candy and wave at the queen's court and Dad would join them, and everyone would act as if nothing were wrong.

Amber walked down the hall to the kitchen at the back of the house. The dishwasher splashed, and she saw the white back of a staff member getting the mop out of the closet. Amber opened the back door and closed it again, softly; but it didn't matter, because somebody in the street was honking furiously. The street and every parking lot for miles were jammed.

Amber walked across the yard, past the cinder-block offices, across the parking lot to a chain-link fence. She was over it in two steps, and in the thick huisache of the Haunted Lot.

The kids in the Center said that strange lights and noises came from the lot at night, but Amber knew what to think of those stories. Older kids could always get hold of a little pot or beer, and the Haunted Lot was the only decent hiding place within sneaking distance of the Center. With no clear idea of what she intended, she picked her way between the yellow-blooming fronds of huisache, the prickly beginnings of sunflowers, and the inevitable broken bottles and windblown papers. Her eyes stung—from the smoke in the air, no doubt—and her glasses slid down

12

her nose. Dad had promised her contact lenses in the fall, for her thirteenth birthday.

She came to a ring of limestone, embraced and enclosed by the roots of an enormous tree stump. She could smell water and feel cooler air above the dark central hole. A well. Amber stretched her legs along the rim of the well, heels braced on the encircling roots, back against the ragged stump. The huisache was tall enough to hide the street. No litter marred the immediate vicinity, but the open maw of the well gaped as handily as a trash can— she didn't like to think of what might be down there.

If she looked up she could see the elevated highway and the Center's red roof against the overcast sky. If she looked down, and blotted out the street sounds, she could pretend it was a hundred years ago.

A hundred years ago, she thought, rubbing under her glasses, everybody had big two-story houses and lots of kids. And none of the kids had to go to shelters because there weren't any drugs and things to turn them delinquent or make their parents beat them up. Even if somebody got orphaned she'd move in with relatives, or get adopted like Anne in *Anne of Green Gables*. Mothers didn't work at anything but being mothers, and nobody ever got divorced, or even separated.

Dad was considering a job that would move him to Austin. He and Mom had argued about it. "You'll be part of the problem, not the solution!" she had yelled one night when they thought Amber was asleep; and he had yelled back, "So what's the solution?"

Mom was considering putting in for a promotion. Dad thought it was a bad idea. "You think if you move another rung up the ladder you'll be able to manipulate the system

13

better," he'd told Mom over Amber's head at dinner one evening, "but there isn't any system. It's a mess."

"Don't tell me what I think," Mom had answered, and asked Amber to pass the potatoes.

Amber didn't see how an argument about where to live or what job to do could be as big a problem as—as the problems people got divorced for. But if Dr. Cunningham was right—Amber took off her glasses and rubbed the sweat off her nose.

Somebody giggled.

"Who's there?" The giggle had been behind the stump, but when she looked, nothing was there. Only a lizard streaked away. Amber snapped open her purse. "I've got a knife," she lied, putting her hand inside, "and I take self-defense."

She heard a splash, and, when she looked, saw two wet footprints no longer than the tip of her index finger smudging the limestone.

Rap music throbbed in the street.

Amber had read *Alice in Wonderland*, and seen the Narnia stories on public television. I'm dreaming, she thought; but the mess of bills, change, candy, and Kleenex in her purse did not feel like a dream. Something radical will happen, she thought; but the world was still.

"Come out, come out, wherever you are!" she called softly, raising a muffled echo and a distant giggle from the depths. She fumbled out a penny and dropped it in, waiting for the *plunk*. "I wish," she began, bending over the invisible water.

The penny hurtled back up out of the well and past her face. Amber pressed herself against the stump, staring at the ring of limestone.

"A-a-amber!" called Mom.

Impulsively Amber snatched an atomic fireball out of her purse, popped it out of its wrapping, and leaned over the well, so far that gravity tugged at her high-riding hair ribbon. "I wish," she gabbled, dropping the round cinnamon candy, "I wish I lived a hundred years ago!"

Plunk! said the water, far below.

And the world fell silent.

CHAPTER THREE

Battle of Flowers, 1991

The air was like a blanket that had been burned and then doused with warm water. The tree was replaced by a stump, the stillness by a bewildering racket, half roar and half pulse. "A-a-amber!" shouted someone. "Amber, where are you?" Only the drying footprints on the edge of the well remained.

Ada's home had been replaced by a large blue building with no windows. Beyond and above the Streichers' familiar red roof reared an enormous bridge, along which objects too fast and bright to identify flashed at frightening speed.

Ada stood, her limbs shaking. If this was a hundred years in the future, it didn't look the way she'd pictured it. But then, people in 1791, she encouraged herself, could never have pictured gaslight and the telephone. After all, she could get back whenever she pleased. All she needed was candy, and she had plenty of money to buy that with. She must go exploring, not stand like a stump.

The path by which she'd come to the well had vanished,

grown over completely. She struggled through the hui-sache and mesquite as best she could. Twice she almost stepped on broken glass, and by the time she found the street she was sticky with heat and had a round hole in her white stocking. She reached into her pocket for her handkerchief to wipe her forehead, but couldn't find it. Annoyance flickered across her mind.

Huge metal boxes, the size of coaches but lower slung, lined up nose to tail on the street, generating foul-smelling air as they inched along. Ada could see people inside them. Why didn't they open their windows? she wondered. On a day like this they must be half cooked! The street was bordered by a low curb and paved flat with some black substance. The Streicher house and the white one across from it were the only familiar things in sight; no china trees, no other neighbors. Ada went toward the blue building.

It had no windows, only a glass door, and the paved-over yard was half filled with metal vehicles. A Mexican boy a little older than Ada held up a hand-printed sign: PARADE PARKING, $2.00. He grinned at her, calling: "Hey, I like your outfit!" He wore practically nothing—a sleeveless shirt and trousers that didn't even cover his knees. Ada hurried on with her eyes averted.

Around the corner she found herself caught in a stream of people. The children seemed to be out in their under-clothes. The men wore no collars, no hats, and no coats; just short trousers and thin shirts with short sleeves. Only a few of the grown-up women approached respectability, and even they wore short skirts better suited to someone Matilda's age.

Dress reform, thought Ada hopefully. Still, sensible as the outfits might be, they were embarrassing to look at. She became even more embarrassed when she realized she was the only white person in sight.

"You're going the wrong way!" shouted a fat woman at someone. "Downtown's the other side of the highway!"

Ada looked up. Highway. The name made more sense for this elevated road than for one at ground level. The flow of the crowd carried her underneath and out the other side, where she finally got a look at the manner of place she was in.

Ada stopped dead. This couldn't be San Antonio! It couldn't be any place in the real world, not with buildings as tall as that! They were tall enough to punch a hole in the sky! Why, you'd burst your lungs climbing to the top of them!

Responding to some signal she didn't catch, all the vehicles in the street stopped and all the people on the curb stepped in front of them. She hurried across, feeling that if she could stop and study things, something would make sense. That big poster, for instance:

IMAX THEATER

ALAMO: THE PRICE OF FREEDOM

and the picture of a man in a coonskin cap—she wanted to stop and look, but the crowd was in a hurry, so she thought she should be in a hurry, too. The tall buildings eclipsed one another as she moved, changing the view with each step, so that she could not feel as if she were really anywhere.

When the crowd stopped rushing forward and started spreading out, she was further convinced that she couldn't be in San Antonio. This plaza was nowhere she'd ever

18

been, with its huge white monument, tiers of metal bleachers, the central green space almost hidden by people. She
squeezed against a limestone wall, trying to catch her
breath as she made her way farther into the plaza, walking
under wooden-barred windows.

The wall ended at a corner. Set well back from the rest
of the plaza, behind a crowd of indecently dressed people,
was the familiar facade of the Alamo. Someone had torn
down the warehouse that should be where she was standing, and taken away the post office. She turned to look at
the building at the north side of the plaza. POST OFFICE AND
FEDERAL BUILDING said the lettering above its door. Not
taken away. Replaced.

For a minute Ada was indignant. *That* building had been
brand-new, and much prettier than this one! Then her
heart began to flutter. She was having a real adventure
and must make the most of it!

Seeing people climbing up the open metal seating, Ada
did the same, settling herself near the top. A hatless
woman was explaining to her children that the parade they
were about to see had been an annual event for a century.
"They call it the Battle of Flowers," she said, "because in
the first one, people decorated their carriages with flowers
and threw them at each other. And it has been getting
bigger and fancier every year since then."

One in the eye for Billy Streicher! thought Ada. She was
too busy trying to pick out the changes (the Menger Hotel
still stood, but a wax museum occupied the site of the
Grand Opera House) to be bored waiting for the parade to
begin; and once that happened, she was dazzled.

Large flat floats filled with waving people and decorated
with fantastic scenes drifted mysteriously by, without

19

horses pulling them. Bands marched in precise formation, performing maneuvers in front of the Alamo. Cavalcades of horses, clowns, enormous balloons, and the metal vehicles—which she heard people around her referring to as cars, as if they were part of a railroad train—passed in endless streams. At intervals came other floats, each carrying one girl in an incredible dress. These, she learned by listening, were the queen and her court of duchesses, crowned last night so they could ride in the parade today. Ada's arm got tired of waving back at the people on the floats, and her mouth was as dry as her skin was wet. People around her bought lemonade from vendors below, but she was squeezed in tight and didn't want to lose her place. I wish Odett were here, she thought. I could send her to buy lemonade. And she'd love the floats.

By the time the sounds of the last band had faded, Ada's mouth was so dry she felt that she would spit cotton, if she were to be so rude as to spit. She went to the nearest lemonade vendor and pulled out a nickel. "One, please."

"One dollar," said the vendor, ladling pale liquid into flimsy cups.

Ada gaped. "A dollar!"

"Yes, a dollar." The lady looked at her, then down at her nickel. "Hey, get out of here with your play money!"

Feeling as if she had been hit in the head, Ada stepped aside. The lady behind her paid up without a murmur, using narrow pieces of green paper money.

The adventure turned nightmarish as Ada tried to find a way through the crowd. Stores and eating houses (some familiar, some strange) lined the plaza opposite the Alamo, one with a sign out declaring itself HOME OF THE $3.98 STEAK DINNER, as if this exorbitant rate were something to be proud of. Nobody paid any attention to her. Her head and feet began to ache.

At Commerce Street Bridge she looked down at the river. Someone had laid walks along the sides, built a couple of arched bridges, and set out tables, reminding her of pictures of Paris. She looked for the Scholz Palm Garden, where Pappa took the family on special occasions, but it had vanished. So had the Hertzberg clock. So had— she began to feel dizzy, looking for things she couldn't find. The Clifford Building, with its tower, still stood, at least. She went closer, looking in the window.

The first thing she saw was an old shield nickel like one she had in her purse, on a card with a price tag. Seventy dollars? Maybe she was saved! Ada squared her shoulders, and went up the steps into air as cold as the refrigerator on the day the iceman came. While the salesclerk tried to sell earrings to a man, Ada studied prices. Eleven dollars for this penny, six dollars and two bits for that—she couldn't make sense of this.

The customer left without buying, and the clerk turned to Ada, unhopefully. She had to swallow twice before her mouth would work. "Excuse me, sir," she said. "I was wondering. I saw a nickel in your window, and you've got it for sale for seventy dollars. Why would anyone pay so much for a nickel?"

"That's what we call a collectible coin," said the clerk.

"People collect nickels?" She had heard of collecting coins, but she'd thought that meant really old ones, made by Greeks and Romans.

"Sure. It's a very interesting hobby." He smiled at her. "Even a kid your age could get started on it."

Ada took her purse out of her pocket, relieved. She'd

21

purchase a drink, explore, buy a piece of candy for the thing in the well, go home when she was ready—and have lots of money for the next visit! "I have some old coins," she said. "Do you buy them?"

"Well . . . the boss would have to do the actual buying. And you'd have to bring your parents in." He pointed to a sign: ALL ITEMS SOLD REQUIRE DRIVER'S LICENSE OR DPS ID CARD; MINIMUM AGE EIGHTEEN. He held out his hand anyway. "I can give you an idea of what they're worth."

Ada had no idea what a DPS ID card was, but she knew she couldn't pass for eighteen. Maybe some other place would be less picky, though. She opened her purse and poured the money onto the countertop. Bronze pennies, nickels, silver dimes—the clerk's eyes lit up at the sight, but as he sorted through them the light faded. At last he shook his head. "I wish I had good news for you, sugar. There's no point showing these to the boss."

"But—this one is like the one in the window." She pushed forward the shield nickel.

"It's the same kind of coin, but look here." He picked it up. "You see where the numbers are almost unreadable? That makes it a poor-condition coin. Nobody wants those except kids—no offense. Your dimes are better-looking than a lot of dimes you see lying around—real good, for a kid's collection. They were pure silver in those days, and the metal's so soft they got real beaten up during regular use. These still don't come up to collectible grade, though." He scooped them all back into her purse. "I bet you could make a good trade with somebody your own age, though."

"Oh," said Ada. "Thank you." She picked up the purse.

"I'm sorry I couldn't do more for you." He smiled apologetically. "You look pretty strung out. You okay?"

Ada hesitated. What did *okay* and *strung out* mean? "I'm
. . . a little thirsty, thank you."

"Hang on." He went through a door into the back and returned with a broad-bottomed mug. "Is water okay?"

Okay must mean "all right," or something like it. Ada said, "Yes, please," and drank. Then there was nothing to do but thank him again, and leave.

Cars crowded the streets and people crowded the walks. Trolleys passed on rubber wheels, instead of rails; and cars so huge that they must be omnibuses roared and groaned. She walked all the way to Military Plaza, hoping to hire herself to a chili queen pouring her spicy soup straight from the pot or a farmer selling vegetables; but the market was nowhere to be seen. The city hall they'd been building last time she'd been here had replaced it entirely. A carnival had been set up behind San Fernando Cathedral, but none of the vendors wanted a girl to lend a hand.

Ada walked back to Main Plaza. At least San Fernando Cathedral was the same; but the gaudy red courthouse to the south and the towering brick building on the north seemed to glare at her as if they knew she didn't belong.

Someone had set up a group of bronze cardplayers. On first catching sight of them, Ada had thought them real; they looked so natural, with their painted clothing and sweaters hanging over the backs of their chairs. People would look over their shoulders, rub the bald statue's head, and make delighted comments to one another. Several times people posed with the figures while friends pointed tiny black boxes at them. It was only after hearing various of these friends instructed to "Take my picture" that Ada came to understand that the black boxes were cameras.

Simpson would have loved it. If only he were here!

The light began to shift into evening, and dinner seemed a long time ago. Ada rested her aching head in her hands, trying to plan. The streets were so clean here that nobody would pay to have the crossing swept for them; and in any case she had no broom. None of the vendors wanted a helper. She would rather die than beg or steal. Perhaps the fairy, or whatever it was in the well, would accept something other than candy. As hot as it was, mulberries might well be getting ripe. If she could find a mulberry tree, perhaps the fruit would work. If only the air were less thick! She was beginning to choke, and her eyes started to sting.

"Are you all right?"

Ada looked up, blinking. The man who had spoken smiled at her kindly. His teeth were flawless. "Are you lost?" he asked.

"I suppose I am, in a way," said Ada. She wondered how much she could tell him. Perhaps time travel was something people in the future did constantly, and he would not be surprised to find out where she was from.

"And I bet you're hungry," said the man. "What say I buy you a hot dog and you tell me all about it?"

Ada could only nod. The man went to a cart on the other side of the plaza and bought a pink sausage laden with mustard and tomato catsup, a shiny bag of Sarasota chips, and a can whose sweet contents fizzed all the way to her belly.

Ada made up her mind. This man was kind and helpful, and it would be unfair to tell him lies or half-truths. He listened quietly as she told him what had happened, in between bites of hot dog and chips. About midway through he put his hand on her shoulder, which made her uncomfortable; but she thought it might be rude to move away. He watched her face so intently that she had a hard time meeting his eyes.

"You do have a problem, don't you?" he said, when she finished. "Here's what we'll do. I'll give you a candy bar and drive you back to that well."

"Oh, would you, sir?" His grip on her shoulder tightened slightly. Ada remembered her obligations, and looked at the empty chip bag in her lap. "You're very kind. I'll come back as soon as ever I can, and I'll pay you back. I promise I will."

He showed his flawless teeth again. "Maybe we can find a way for you to pay me off." He stood up, removing his hand from her shoulder a moment later. "My car's over this way."

"Shouldn't we get the candy first?" asked Ada, shaking the crumbs from her lap. A bin for trash stood near the fountain—a tip-top idea, that!—but it was overflowing, and she had to balance her refuse on top of the pile.

"None of these people sell candy fit for a wishing fairy," said the man. "I have some at home that'll be just what we need." He took her hand, clammily.

Ada felt too old for hand holding; but after all, he was rescuing her. He led her toward a paved lot crammed with cars.

"Hi there," said a policeman, stepping across their path.

She could tell he was a policeman, despite the strange cut of his uniform, by the badge on his pocket. "Haven't seen you in a while, George."

The man stopped, his smile suddenly stiff and dead. "Uh . . . hi," he said, taking half a step back and squeezing Ada's hand so tightly it hurt. "My niece and I were just, uh . . ."

Ada gaped at him. Why would he tell such a fib?

"Your niece, huh?" said the policeman. "Is that right, kid? Is this your uncle?"

Ada opened her mouth and closed it again. This nice man must have some reason for telling such a story. On the other hand, to lie to a policeman—

"What's his name?" pressed the policeman.

"I don't . . . I don't know, sir," Ada admitted.

Her rescuer looked desperate. "Ada, what do you want to lie like that for? You know my name perfectly well."

"So do I," said the policeman, "and I'm telling you to leave her alone. Or do you want to go on back to jail?"

George dropped Ada's hand and walked away. Ada stared after him. "They don't like child molesters in our jail," said the policeman in a contented tone. "Last time we had him in, he came out black and blue. Didn't your folks ever teach you not to talk to strangers, kid?"

"No, sir," said Ada. Not neat strangers with perfect teeth, at any rate!

"Where'd you leave your parents?"

"In 1891," said Ada.

The policeman sighed. "Okay. Fine. I'll call the station and see if anyone's come looking for you. What's your name?"

He led her out of the main flow of foot traffic, took a black oblong object off his belt, and spoke into it. "Got a lost child here," he said. "About twelve years old, brown hair, brown eyes, say four foot nine, wearing a green dress. Says her name is Ada Bauer." Fuzzy sounds crackled from the box. It must be some kind of portable telephone! "Well, this one's playing games. Says she left her parents in 1891." Fuzz and crackling. "Yeah, I bet. You page her old man." He put the telephone back on his belt. "Come on, honey. Your folks have been looking for you."

Ada fell into step beside him. "But they can't have!"

"We'll just have to hold you till they show up, then."

She thought she saw the Hertzberg clock in an unexpected place as he led her through the pavement maze, but she was too tired to try to recognize things anymore. If only Mamma and Pappa could be at the police station!

A man leaped up when they came in, took two steps toward them, and stopped. "Mr. Burak?" asked the policeman.

"Yes," he said, "but that's not Amber."

"My parents won't be here, sir." Ada curtsied. "They're"—the idea made her feel hollow and lonesome—"dead."

Mr. Burak looked at her as if trying to focus through a fog. He was clean shaven, but rumpled and hatless. "Your parents are dead? Both of them?"

"Yes, sir," said Ada. "They must be, by now."

"Where are you staying?"

"Nowhere, sir."

"I bet she's run away from a foster home," said Mr. Burak to the policeman. "About Amber . . ." Losing interest in Ada, he told the policeman all about Amber, where she had been lost, at what time. Ada sat down in an orange chair of some hard material.

Mr. Burak went away. The policeman turned her over to a woman in a uniform. Ada answered her questions truthfully, but the woman did not seem satisfied. She was kind, in a brusque way; and when she learned that Ada had a headache, she brought her pills and some water. After the questions were answered, though, Ada was forgotten as the policemen and women dealt with other, mostly disreputable, people.

No one noticed Ada again until the street outside was dark, and Mr. Burak came in with a woman who looked as worn out as a laundress, though she wore a festive embroidered frock. They talked to the policewoman, and turned away with slumping shoulders; at which point the woman saw Ada. She asked Mr. Burak something, then returned to the desk and talked to the policewoman again.

Ada was too well-bred to eavesdrop; but she could not help hearing when the woman raised her voice. "You can't send her there! That place is a hellhole!" *Murmur, murmur, murmur.* "Of course I can. It's my job!" *Murmur, murmur, murmur.* "Yes, yes, I'll sign whatever you like. Give it here."

After some business with printed papers, the policewoman led them over. "Ada, this is Mrs. Burak," she said. "She's going to take you someplace to stay tonight. You ready?"

"Yes, ma'am." Ada stood up, unsteady, and curtsied.

Mrs. Burak smiled shakily and shook Ada's hand as if she were a grown woman. "We're taking you to an emergency shelter," she said. "It's a place where we keep kids like you until we find the best way to take care of them. It's crowded, but it's clean, and there's nothing to be afraid of. Will you come?"

"Yes, ma'am," Ada said. What choice did she have?

Mr. and Mrs. Burak led her, not outside, but farther into the building. Except for the police station and a couple of shops on the first floor, the whole place appeared to have been built to store those ever-present cars. Ada hesitated when Mr. Burak opened the rear door of one for her, but Mrs. Burak slid into the front with every sign of confidence, and Ada followed suit. Inside the air was stifling; but when Mr. Burak turned a key in a wheel mounted in the front, something roared softly, and cool air started blowing. Seeing the Buraks strap themselves in, Ada followed suit, struggling with the buckles as the car moved— down and around, down and around, and out into the street.

"We'll have to go back for your car," said Mr. Burak.

"The number fifteen bus goes right by Streicher," said Mrs. Burak. "I can do it by myself."

"You think Amber might go back to the car?"

"I've got the staff on alert for her." Mrs. Burak made a sound as if she were about to cry. Mr. Burak held the wheel with one hand and rested the other on the back of her neck. Ada, embarrassed, watched the dark world flash by outside the window. Soon they drove up an incline and onto the highway, into a moving stream of red lights. A similar stream of white lights traveled in the other direction. Ada felt as though they were floating.

She was half asleep when the car stopped. Mrs. Burak

left and returned, muttering about idiots and bureaucrats. "It's all settled," she said. "C'mon, Ada. They've found a bed for you."

"Where?" asked Mr. Burak, not moving from behind the wheel.

"That pregnant girl with Violet decided to go home."

"Are you sure that's a good idea?"

"It'll be educational. Besides, there isn't anyplace else."

Ada got the straps undone and slid out of the car. Mrs. Burak led her to a porch, to a hall, where a cross-looking woman waited. Mrs. Burak bent down to be on a level with Ada's face. "Loyce will take you till we find a permanent place. Okay?"

"Yes, ma'am." Ada nodded. "I hope you find your little girl soon."

Mrs. Burak's face flickered like a dying candle. "Thanks, Ada," she said breathlessly, and left.

CHAPTER FOUR

Battle of Flowers, 1891

Shade danced on Amber's sundress. Someone called: "A-a-ada! Where are you?"

A mockingbird trilled in the tree that a moment before had been a stump. Tiny footprints dried on the well's rim. Amber could see the red roof of the Streicher Children's Center, backed only by blue sky and white cloud. A fly buzzed past her nose.

"I did it!" whispered Amber.

"Ada!" The person calling was getting fed up. "Stop it! You know you're to mind Toby and Doris this afternoon!"

Two paths led out from the well through the huisache, one toward the Center, one toward the voice. Ada went toward the Center. The playground had been replaced by a rose garden. All the windows stood open, the lower ones covered by heavy screens, the upper ones with curtains dancing in and out freely. Without the highway, the backyard was big enough to hold an extra building—a real live carriage house!

Amber twirled, trying to take in everything at once.

Umbrella-shaped chinaberry trees shaded the unpaved street. The clinic across the street was a private house, without bus stop or parking lot. That funky-looking blue warehouse had been replaced by a white house with a tin roof. Wooden poles lined the cross street, draped with power lines.

A teenage girl with thick brown hair tied at the nape of her neck stood in front of the white house, her hands cupped around her mouth. "A-a-a-ada!" Her dress was not much longer than Mom wore her skirts (Mom hated the way her legs looked and covered them up as much as she could), but the girl wore high-buttoned boots and long sleeves. When she saw Amber, the teenager called: "Hi! Have you seen my little sister?"

"No," said Amber, suddenly conscious of her sundress. She reached up to fiddle with her hair, which flopped loosely—her ribbon had come out somewhere.

The teenager sighed, started to turn away, then turned back. "You get along home, yourself," she said, in a strong accent. "You should be ashamed, cavorting around in your underthings!"

Amber didn't see what business it was of hers, but ran off without saying so. She would have to rip something off (temporarily, of course) from a clothesline to cover her sundress.

This took longer than it should have. Amber ducked down the first alley she came to, so as to have a good view of backyards and keep out of sight. Yards and houses both were bigger than she was used to. All the yards had clotheslines, but most were empty, or sported only rows of square white cloths, too small to do Amber any good. (Later she figured out that they were cloth diapers.) Of course, back before anybody had washers and dryers, nobody who could afford to pay someone else to do it would wash her own clothes. It would be too much work. Amber was beginning to feel annoyed and a little desperate when, among some smaller, poorer houses several blocks from her starting point, she had the luck to happen upon a washerwoman's house, its grassless yard crisscrossed with clotheslines flapping with bright skirts. Amber felt both guilty and triumphant as she nipped over the fence, grabbed a yellow dress, and nipped back undetected.

Heading back the way she had come, she found a narrow shed she could get into unobserved, and slipped in to dress properly. Ooh, it stunk! Just like the outhouse that time Dad had taken her camping in the Hill Country.

In fact, she realized, as she adjusted to the light, it *was* an outhouse. Gross! She tried not to breathe as she arranged her clothes. The skirt covered her sundress with room to spare. The top part was enough too big for her that she could hide her purse just by buttoning the dress up (way too many buttons!) over it.

Amber emerged from the outhouse feeling more secure, found her way back to a street, and realized she had no idea where she was. Every way she looked she saw dirt streets, chinaberry trees, wooden and stone houses, power lines, and children playing in yards. There weren't even any street signs.

A group of boys in vests, knee pants, and hats played marbles in the street nearby, and some girls clustered on a porch like petunias having a doll's tea party. She approached the boys, since they were closer. "Hey," she said, "excuse me, but I'm a little turned around here. Can you tell me where I am?"

The boys looked up. One of them hooted. "Turned around! I wouldn't boast about it if I were you!"

"Who's boasting?" asked Amber. "I'm asking directions."

"North, south, east, west," said one boy.

"No wonder you're lost," said another. "You're going backward."

They all had strong accents, like people from the country.

Amber sized them up, trying to pick out the leader. Probably the biggest boy, standing in the back saying nothing, but watching everything. She spoke straight at him. "Are you monkeys always this rude, or is the zookeeper gone today?"

He smiled a superior smile, and swept his hat off in a deep bow. "Oh, forgive us our uncouthness, great lady of the land! How may your humble servants assist you?"

"For starters, you can answer my question," said Amber, longing to knock the hat out of his hand and the grin off his face. "Where am I?"

"Nolan Street, District One, San Antonio, Texas, United States of America, North American continent, Western Hemisphere, the Earth, the Universe!"

The other boys laughed. The girls had stopped their tea party to listen. Amber ignored them. "And how do I get downtown from here?"

"Walk!" suggested the smallest boy.

Amber took a deep breath, but was interrupted before she ever began. The teenage girl she had seen before came down the street so fast she was almost running, and pounced on the biggest boy. "Billy! Have you seen Ada anywhere?"

"Not since we all walked home," said Billy.

"She excused herself from the table early and nobody's seen her since! She was supposed to mind the little ones this afternoon, and she knew we were counting on her." The teenager seemed more worried now, and less exasperated. "We can't imagine where she's gotten to. Have any of y'all seen her?"

The girls came down from the porch in answer to this plea, but neither they nor the boys had seen anything. Not until she had extracted a denial of knowledge from Amber along with the rest did the teenager recognize her. "Are you certain?" she asked, looking Amber up and down with restrained curiosity. "You were there about the time she disappeared. She's more or less your age, with brown hair and a green dress, and no hat."

"You were the first person I saw," said Amber.

"Have you checked the well in the Haunted Lot?" piped up the youngest boy, then quailed at the look Billy gave him.

"Don't be a little donk! Ada's too big to tumble down the well!" Billy turned to the teenager with a bright, reassuring face. "I'll tell you what it is. She was in a fearful temper about the way Miss Grundage treated her essay this morning, and you know how high-horse she can get about having to mind the kids. She's gone to have a sulk somewhere and is laying low. She'll show up in time for the parade—you'll see, Matilda."

"If she does she won't get to see it," said Matilda decidedly. "She'll be lucky if she doesn't get switched!"

"When is the parade?" asked Amber. She had forgotten all about the Battle of Flowers—but she'd been on her way to the hundredth one when she'd gotten sidetracked, so if she'd gone back a hundred years, they must be about to have the first one!

"Five o'clock," said Billy, "but you'll never find it."

"Try walking backward," snickered one of the smaller boys.

"You should be ashamed of yourself," snapped Matilda, "making fun of a poor girl that way! You didn't have anyone to help you button that, did you?" she asked Amber.

"No," said Amber, beginning to suspect what was wrong.

"Well, come along of me and I'll help you with." Matilda, apparently thinking this was an understandable sentence, set off as quickly as she had come. Amber followed gratefully. They stepped behind a hedge, unbuttoned the dress, and turned it around without taking it off. If Matilda noticed anything odd underneath the dress, she was too polite to say so. "They aren't bad boys, you know, just thoughtless," said Matilda, buttoning the yellow dress down the back. "I haven't seen you before. Where are you staying?"

"I'm just passing through," said Amber. "Can you tell me how to get downtown?"

"Straight down this street, and turn left after you cross the ditch. Haven't you a hat, or stockings?"

"I'm fine." Amber knew the tone of Matilda's voice; she sounded like Mom, about to start delving into somebody else's kid's problems. The last thing Amber needed was people interrupting her adventure to take care of her. As soon as the last button was fastened, she moved away. "Thanks a bunch. I have to go. Hope you find Ada soon."

She hurried off, but soon slowed down. Though not as hot as the day she had started with, it was way too warm to wear two dresses. Also, she didn't want to miss anything. By 1991 this whole neighborhood had been pretty much replaced by warehouses, and on every hand (ignoring the mess left by horses and the totally unreasonable number of flies) she could see the superior beauty of 1891. The yards were full of flowers and girls in hats and flowerlike dresses. The ladies looked neat and stately, with their hair piled up on their heads and their long, light dresses. The boys looked dorky and the men stuffy, but so did the men and boys she'd known all her life. You couldn't expect anything else from them. Next time, she thought, waving a fly away from her face, I'll wear Off. And I bet I can dress up right if I try.

She had known San Antonio used to be smaller, but she was astonished at just how much smaller it was. She was practically to the Alamo before she stopped seeing single-family houses, or started seeing paved streets. Some of these were paved only at the crosswalks, and the paving was mostly wood blocks, on which the steel tires of the horse-drawn vehicles made a surprising amount of racket. The traffic didn't seem to have any rules, either. Once in a while a brightly colored trolley car came down a set of rails in the middle of a street, clanging a bell, and everyone, including the horses, got out of the way; but otherwise, it seemed, you were on your own.

In some places Amber could see farther than she was used to, since no building was more than four stories tall; in others, the view was blocked by crowded power lines. Many buildings were as frilly and fancy as she had expected; but a surprisingly large number were squat and ugly, covered with posters for medicine that cured "female complaints," whatever those were.

People were everywhere, and all busy—boys polishing

37

people's shoes (which needed it badly, there was so much dirt even on the paved streets), people selling candy and tamales and bird cages, and even a real live blacksmith. She wasn't the only child to gather around his door; but she was practically the only girl, and she had to do a little of what Mom called self-assertion and the teachers called shoving to get her right to watch properly recognized.

Alamo and Main plazas looked bare, with new-looking trees and grass. Military Plaza was practically unrecognizable. City Hall stood half-built in the center, its sides covered with scaffolding, glaring white. Amber had been here with Mom on errands to the city offices a couple of times, and the plaza had always been pretty quiet; but now it was packed. It was a market! Women with wicker baskets picked their way through crowded tables, buying fruits and vegetables and even meat, as if they were at a grocery store.

By this time Amber was a bit tired and munchy. She had eaten a smallish lunch, planning on cotton candy and popcorn at the parade. Now the smell of food made her feel hollow. Her purse was a useless lump under her dress. Her paper money looked nothing like what people were paying with around here, and some of her coins had images of presidents who hadn't been born yet on them; she couldn't possibly buy anything. She had her atomic fireballs, but they were all flavor and no filling.

She stood and watched for a while, trying to get a line on her options. Every time a new woman appeared with a basket, boys besieged her with offers to carry it as she shopped, and every time one delivered a full basket safely to a waiting buggy, he got a nickel. Amber decided to go into business for herself.

This was easier to think of than to do. Although it seemed to her that there were plenty of shoppers to go around, the boys made it clear they didn't want her horning in; and the ladies she approached seemed shocked to see her. Finally she noticed one fussy woman shooing away all the boys on the grounds that they were dirty. Approaching her with relatively clean hands, and a story about wanting a nickel to buy candy for an imaginary crippled sister (all those old-fashioned books she'd read paying off), she was, to her relief, hired.

Even this had its drawbacks. The woman was every bit as fussy with the vendors as she had been with the boys, so filling the basket took forever. Then, Amber found, they had to walk all the way to the woman's house, practically back to the Alamo and several blocks north, because she didn't have a buggy, and was too cheap to take the streetcar.

To Amber's surprise, however, when they were almost at their destination, the woman bought two conical brown candies, called *peloncillos*, and gave them to her along with her nickel: one for her, and the other for her crippled sister. "It's kind of you to think of your sister, but don't forget, you need things, too," she said, standing on the steps of a small, pretty house. "If you'll take my advice, you'll give her the *peloncillo* and save the nickel toward some decent shoes! Good afternoon."

She opened the door without unlocking it, and went in, leaving Amber to stick the nickel in her pocket and go off down the street with a *peloncillo* in each hand. Well, that was more than she'd needed! But how did these things taste? She put the tip of one cone into her mouth. Not bad—like brown sugar.

Feeling better, but with sore feet, she decided she would see the parade and then go home. At one of the major streets a trolley came by so slowly that she was able to hitch a ride on the back. The conductor caught her almost at once; but it turned out the fare was five cents, so she spent her hard-earned money for a ride to Alamo Plaza.

Downtown was more crowded than it had been. Someone had put a star made of branches in the top of the Alamo facade, and the balcony of the building next door, where the renovated mission buildings would be, was full of people. Bleachers didn't seem to have been invented yet, so Amber sat on the curb.

Amber gave one of her *peloncillos* to a little barefoot girl who seemed to be all by herself, and sucked on the other till the sugar melted to nothing in her mouth. It must be after five by now. Why didn't they close the streets? Carriages were still trying to force their way into the plaza. She hoped she'd be able to see something when the parade finally came. Right now the whole world seemed to consist of pantlegs and skirts.

Finally she heard cheering, and fought her way to her feet. Yes! Here they came—buggies with mounds of flowers in their seats, horses with roses in their harness pulling women and children and more flowers; roses and bluebonnets and mountain laurel and—Amber had no idea what most of the blossoms were called, but they were all over everything. They twined in the spokes of buggy wheels and hid the bridles and saddles of high-stepping horses ridden by young men dressed in white and black. A cavalcade of bicycles (which received great cheers, especially the lone woman) left streams of petals fluttering in its wake. A broken-down buggy drawn by a skinny horse, labeled POOR BUT IN IT, had flowers as fat and pretty as the ones on the biggest float, which carried a bower full of young ladies who Amber guessed must be the first queen's court, though their dresses were plain white and the girls were all sharing one float. Everyone laughed and cheered and shouted.

Amber had to jump up and down to see everything. Policemen on horses were directing traffic now, sending half the buggies around one side of the plaza and the other half to the other. Someone was shouting orders, but she couldn't make out the words. The battle began.

The two sides drove back and forth pelting each other with the mounds of flowers piled on their floats. The bikes and the people on horseback wove in and out between the less-maneuverable buggies. People in the crowd clapped and cheered for their friends. The children on an all-white float threw their flowers so inexpertly that they didn't hit anyone except by accident, but the women in the bower defended themselves against all comers with deadly accuracy.

A boy ran out, picked up a fallen rose, and hurled it at the children with a shout. Another boy ran out. Then another. Amber grabbed a branch of laurel and ran out too, dodging wheels and hooves. She ducked and threw and ran, scooping blossoms from the ground to hurl at whoever was handy. This was great! Why had they ever taken the "battle" out of "Battle of Flowers"?

A fistfight that erupted in front of the Menger Hotel reminded her. In her day, those wouldn't be fists; they'd be knives. She didn't want to think about that now. She wanted to score a hit on the bicycling woman.

She was pursuing this ambition near Joske's Dry Goods store when a horse ran away. She didn't see what caused it, but suddenly people scattered, and a boy went flying, hit by a wheel. The horse was huge, the buggy behind it swinging wildly from side to side. A small, screaming kid ran in exactly the wrong direction.

Amber did not think. She ran, grabbed the kid by the skirt, and practically threw her out of the way. Something heavy came down on her own skirt. The noise was deafening, but the only pain was where her knee had hit the wooden pavement.

The kid bawled. A dozen hands came down to help Amber to her feet.

"Are you all right?" demanded Matilda.

Amber gulped. "I'm fine. How's the little girl?"

"Boy," corrected Matilda. "He'll be daisy. Mamma—" She turned toward the woman holding the kid, kissing and soothing him—him, in skirts and long curly hair!

Amber ran off into the crowd, still milling in the wake of the horse, which someone had stopped. The boy who'd been knocked flying had a crowd around him; so did another boy who was sitting up. It wasn't hard to get lost.

Her knee hurt something awful. Her purse had twisted around under her dress. It was banging the backs of her legs, and the strap rubbed her shoulder sore. It was time to go home; but that had its own problems. She was still mad at Mom and Dad. They'd be mad at her, too. She worked out what to say to them as she limped through the darkening evening.

She didn't know this part of town very well in her own day; the absence of familiar landmarks and of street signs made the job of finding the Haunted Lot that much harder. She recognized the Streicher Center carriage house, though, and then it was easy.

Lights were coming on in houses up and down the street, and people clustered on the porch of the white one, fussing over the kid she had rescued. Matilda's family must have come straight home. Amber crossed the Streicher rose garden and felt her way along the Haunted Lot till she found an opening in the undergrowth.

In the shelter of the huisache, darkness and mosquitoes and small night noises throve. Afraid that she might fall into the well in the darkness, Amber crawled, her legs tangling in her double layer of skirts and in the strap of her purse. When the live oak loomed above her, she groped until she found the well's wall, and stood up.

Removing the yellow dress was not easy. A couple of buttons she couldn't reach at all, and had to just tear off. She had meant to return it to the washerwoman, but it was such a wreck now that there was no point. She dug in her purse until she found the smooth, round atomic fireballs. Popping one out of its crinkly wrapper, she whispered into the damp darkness: "I wish I could go home, now."

The fireball plunked softly in the distant water. A kitten, or maybe a night bird, mewed somewhere. A man's voice called: "A-a-da!" Amber's knee throbbed. Nothing else happened.

Nothing at all.

She was still too shocked and blank inside to try to hide when, several minutes later, the man looking for Ada came crashing through the huisache, lantern bobbing in his hand, and found her.

CHAPTER FIVE

Violet

Ada's adventure of the previous day was not possible. She had determined this by logic and reason, in the safe confines of her own mind. The odd chill in the air, the absence of Odett's warm breathing, would be accounted for when she opened her eyes, or she didn't know what she would do; so she kept them closed.

A harsh buzz was followed by a click. She heard covers thrown back, feet thump upon the floor, a muffled yawn. Someone tugged at her sheet. "Hey, you, wake up. If you don't get up early, the big girls hog the bathroom."

Ada opened her eyes. "I'm Violet," said a face the color of *peloncillo*. "What do I call you?"

"Ada Bauer." She sat up as Violet began pulling clothes out of a bureau next to the other bed. Mamma would be furious if she knew that Ada had been put in with a person of color. On the other hand, Mrs. Burak had indicated last night that this was the only place to put Ada. She'd best not make a fuss about it.

Ada got out of bed, feeling shy in the thin cotton nightdress that she had been given last night. The bureau next to her bed was empty, and her frock and underthings were not to be found, only her boots and her purse. Even her asafetida bag, which she wore around her neck to ward off smallpox, was gone.

"What's the matter?" asked Violet. "Didn't you have any clothes?"

"Only what I stood up in," said Ada, "and she took those last night."

"Better borrow some of mine." Violet, who had started to shut her drawer, opened it again. "You wear a bra yet?"

"A what?"

"You know, a bra. For your bazooms." Violet held up a flimsy contraption of straps and cloth, and looked critically at Ada's chest. "Yeah, you better."

Ada balked when offered trousers that would not have reached her knees, so Violet, with an audibly tolerant, "Okay, if that's what you want!" found a skirt of acceptable length, made of blue denim, and fastened up the front with an ingenious contrivance, which Violet referred to as a zipper. She also produced a dressing gown, with which Ada covered herself for the trip down the hall to the bathroom.

This room restored her flagging faith in the wonders of the future. She knew that some people had water closets; but this room of gleaming tile and spouts ready to flow freely with water, hot or cold, at the twist of a handle, surpassed her wildest dreams. Violet operated everything with a casual confidence that could only inspire respect.

"They make you shower and brush your teeth before breakfast here," she informed Ada, "which is pretty dumb. This place isn't bad, though." She began arranging her hair in three braids. "Last place I was at, I took one look at the bathroom, and I ran off. You ever been in a shelter before?"

Ada shook her head, struggling to fasten her boots without the aid of a buttonhook.

"Well, they can keep you here up to thirty days, so you better start learning. What you got to remember is, you're on your own. Nobody's going to ask you what you want, so you got to figure out how to get along without that." She paused, snapping a red elastic band around a braid. "Okay, so sometimes the social workers ask you what you want, but mostly they tell you it can't be done. You got to know the rules before you can get around them."

"But I wouldn't want to evade the rules," Ada protested.

"How do you know that, till you know what the rules are?" asked Violet. "Jeez Louise, where'd you get those shoes?"

"Wolfman's," Ada answered without thinking, naming the store where they'd been bought. "They're all I have."

"If anybody makes fun of them, say it's the latest style in California." A knocking on the locked door at that point hurried them out of the bathroom, but Violet's conversation continued to enlighten and instruct Ada all the way down to the dining hall.

In many ways the layout of the house was familiar, as if an ordinary dwelling had been turned into a dormitory. All the rooms were electrically lit, although the sun was well up, and breakfast was served buffet-style in a room full of round white tables. The choices consisted of cold cereal foods and milk in waxed cardboard boxes, and fruit juice in cans. Ada, who had been looking forward to a bowl of

46

grits, concealed her disappointment as best she could and took the same choices Violet did, raisin bran and orange juice. The first to appear, they sat at a table in a corner, and Violet identified everyone who came in in a low voice.

"That's Jennifer taking care of the retarded kids. She's the most okay person on the staff, but don't count on her too much. Stay away from Cody, that white boy over there. He thinks he's hot stuff 'cause his uncle's a pusher and he can get hold of the hard stuff anytime. Even in here. The Bobbsey twins"—indicating a white and a Mexican girl giggling as they selected their breakfast boxes—"are runaways. Be nice to those Mladenka kids. Their mom freaked out when their dad went to jail, and they had to put her in a mental home."

Pusher? Hard stuff? Freaked out? When Violet turned to her and said: "See? Whatever you're here for, it's not any worse than anybody else's problems, so is it okay if I ask you what it is?" Ada was too bewildered to arrange her answer.

"I wished in a well to live a hundred years from—from when I was. What year is it now? It *was* April 24, 1891."

Violet rolled her eyes. "You know, if you don't think it's any of my business, just tell me!"

"It isn't, actually," said Ada, stung. "I notice you haven't told me why you're here."

Violet shrugged. "Look out, here comes Loyce."

The woman who had let Ada in last night approached, looking cross and tired. Ada, embarrassed by Violet's lack of respect, stood up and made her curtsy. "Good morning, Miss Capshaw," she said, clearly, so everyone would know she knew better than to call a grown woman by her first name.

"Morning," said Miss Capshaw, looking at her oddly. "I need you in the office as soon as you finish breakfast." She pointed at a sign on the wall near the buffet. "Those are the house rules, Ada. I want you to read them and remember them."

Ada opened her mouth to reply; but suddenly the younger of the children whose mother had "freaked out" fell out of his chair, screaming incoherently. Miss Capshaw ran over. Ada sat down.

After breakfast Violet led Ada to the front of the building, where she would have expected the parlor to be. Instead, there were two rooms furnished mostly in metal. Here she was taken in hand by a young woman who said to call her Trisha and who sat in front of a dark glass-fronted box tapping an elegantly flat typewriter keyboard. Magically, the glass filled up with letters and lines made of green light.

The second question after her name was Ada's date of birth. Seeing Trisha putting it down wrong, she repeated herself. "August 7, 1878."

Trisha's smile flickered. "Now, don't be silly. That would make you a hundred and thirteen."

"A hundred and twelve," said Ada.

Trisha laughed unconvincingly. "Well, that's an original approach to the problem!" She made her voice serious and persuasive. "I understand that you don't want to be here. And I'm sure you honestly believe that you can take care of yourself. But no matter how old you feel, you're still a minor. We're here to help you, and we can't do it if you play games with us."

"I'm not playing games," said Ada, feeling stubborn. "I was born in 1878."

Trisha's mouth set in a hard line. "If that's the way you want it," she said, punching a button on the keyboard, so that a flashing green light hopped to the next blank line. "Social security number?"

The door opened and a woman breezed in. "Morning, Trisha!" she said, slapping a stack of manila folders onto the desk.

"Thanks, Dr. Cunningham," said Trisha, swiveling her chair. "Are you going to have time to see any kids today?"

Ada stood politely, watching the newcomer with interest. She had never seen a woman doctor before. This one had green-painted eyelids, and shoes with heels three inches high. "I'm already running late," she answered Trisha. "Any urgent cases?"

"The Mladenka kids. Loyce wants them on medication and Grace is fighting her."

"Oh, not Grace again! I'm in enough trouble with her already. Did you hear her kid vanished?"

"Amber?" Trisha looked interested. "What happened?"

"I ran into them at Streicher when they came to collect the kids for the parade, and Grace went upstairs to handle a crisis. So I happened to let on to Amber that I knew about Grace and Lyle splitting up—and would you believe they hadn't told her yet?"

Trisha made a disapproving sound.

"Anyway, she seems to have run off after I talked to her, and Grace is blaming me! I told her, if you aren't honest with your kid I don't see where I'm at fault." Dr. Cunningham picked up a new stack of folders from the top of a cabinet. "Where're those kids? I may as well look before I write the prescription."

"Watching 'Ninja Turtles,' I expect," said Trisha. "Oh,

49

and this is Ada Bauer. You'll have to evaluate her pretty soon."

Dr. Cunningham took notice of Ada for the first time. "Oh? What's your problem, Ada?"

Ada dropped a curtsy. Dr. Cunningham's abrupt manner disturbed her; but she was in favor of female doctors, so this must be all right. "She won't believe me," said Ada, "but I was born in 1878."

Dr. Cunningham lifted one eyebrow. "What year is it now?"

"Nineteen hundred and ninety-one, if the fairy can count." Ada wished she could guess what the doctor was thinking. "I know it sounds improbable, but it's true. Honor bright."

"Honor bright, huh? Is that any relation to Rainbow Brite?"

"I beg your pardon, ma'am?"

"Never mind. You're one for the books, all right, but I don't have time right now." She departed.

Ada answered all questions truthfully, but Trisha was impatient with most of these answers, and angry when Ada could not understand her question about "shots." Released at last, Ada followed the sound of voices to a room, which might have been the rear parlor, furnished as a playroom. Some of the voices came from a box like the one on which Trisha had put Ada's answers. Instead of letters, the glass front displayed moving photographs, in brilliant color, of girls playing with dolls. The other voices belonged to the children.

"I wanna watch Bugs Bunny," said the younger Mladenka child, repeatedly, rhythmically, and without pausing.

"I don't care," said Cody, the boy whose uncle was a pusher. "I already let y'all watch your stupid Ninja Turtles. Now I want to watch wrestling."

"You didn't 'let' anybody do anything," said Violet.

The Mexican "Bobbsey twin" rolled her eyes, sprawling on the divan. "I can't believe we're arguing about what TV show to watch! I might as well be at home."

"I wanna watch Bugs Bunny!"

The moving photos on the box changed—to moving drawings! "We could just watch 'Captain Planet,' " suggested one of the smaller children; but the whole room seemed against her on that. Violet turned a knob on the box. The music changed to something shrill and lively, but her body blocked Ada's view.

Cody took hold of Violet's arm. "I'm tired of you getting in my face."

"I'm tired of you thinking you're the boss of the world," said Violet.

"I could beat you up, you know," he said, jerking her arm.

Ada took a step forward, though she had no idea what she could do if Cody did strike Violet. No one else moved.

"I know," said Violet. "I also know Jennifer'll be back any minute now, and if you're fighting you'll get sent to juvenile hall. And the last time you got sent to juvenile hall you got the snot beat out of you."

"You'll get sent there, too," said Cody.

"Not if you're beating on me and I don't beat back."

"I can't see Bugs Bunny," said the Mladenka boy.

Ada walked across the space between the door and the box, laid her hand on Violet's unoccupied arm, and said, as if nothing were going on, "If y'all don't get out from in front of the picture, he'll never be quiet."

Cody let go of Violet's arm. Violet went with Ada to the divan, not taking her eyes from her foe. Cody made a movement toward the control knob, then another movement away; then Jennifer entered the room with one of her charges, and Cody left.

"What's the matter with him?" asked Jennifer.

"Oh, he's ticked off because he wanted to watch wrestling and we outvoted him," said Violet.

Everyone watched the pictures as a large black-and-white cat attempted to catch a canary with a head like a baseball. Ada leaned over and said into Violet's ear: "Shouldn't we tell her?"

Violet shook her head. "Naw. Nothing happened, really. But thanks for coming in. These other kids have no guts."

This was not the sort of compliment Ada was accustomed to receiving, but she felt sufficiently cast off and alone to value it. She settled down to watch the TV show. The drawings moved and changed with bewildering rapidity, and perhaps Mamma and Pappa would consider the stories vulgar. However, they were fascinating to watch. Moving photographs she found wonderful but not surprising—clearly the TV was a sort of magic lantern, and reproductions in color of moving people must be based on advanced principles of photography—but moving drawings! She could not understand how it was done.

When that show ended, the argument over what to watch next was resolved in favor of a story about a huge ship traveling among the stars. Humanity among the stars! Never in her wildest dreams had Ada considered that possibility. And there on the TV were people from different planets!

It was too much for one morning; and when the Mladenka boy became frightened by the ugliness of the Ferengi captain, Ada volunteered to take him outside. The playground had its own peculiarities, but a sandlot was a sandlot, whatever the date.

That day and the next, Ada received so many minor shocks that she soon ceased to feel them. Sunday morning was marked, not by church, but by fights among the children as to who got to read the "funnies" from the newspaper first. Ada did her best by herself, saying her prayers and scouring the building for a Bible. There was none, though Jennifer promised to loan her one for next Sunday. Next Sunday! Ada could not really believe that she would be here so long.

Violet was a big help, making Ada forget her conscience about playing with a colored girl—no, a black girl. Violet corrected her on that subject vigorously. *Black* was the proper word to use now. Since *black* had been slightly insulting in her day, Ada decided to avoid referring to the matter at all.

Monday morning, dressed uncomfortably in clothing chosen from a "Goodwill box," Ada stood on the porch with the other children waiting for the school bus. She had found a high-necked frock the right length, and stockings that came to her knees. "S'matter, Ada, you think if some guy sees your gorgeous bod he won't be able to control himself?" sneered Cody, flipping her skirt. Ada jumped away, feeling her face burn.

"Leave her alone," said Violet. She wore a vivid pink shirtwaist hanging loose outside her blue denim trousers and had painted her eyelids with some green glittery substance. "Pants are against her religion."

"Oh, sure, Vi." Cody slouched against the porch pillar. "There ain't any religion like that."

"Sure, there is. Jehovah's Witness girls can't wear pants or makeup or nothing. At least she's not trying to convert us."

Jennifer led the retarded children (Ada had decided that *retarded* was the new way to say *feebleminded*) out onto the porch. Cody took a comb out of his pocket and began disarranging his hair. Violet sat on the bottom step with her ring binder in her lap, and Ada sat next to her.

"What's a Jehovah's Witness?" asked Ada softly.

"Jeez! And I thought I had you figured out!" Violet looked disgusted. "If you're not a Jehovah's Witness, what are you?"

"Lutheran," said Ada. "It's not against my religion to wear trousers, but I wouldn't feel decent. Girls didn't wear them—"

"In 1891, I know." Violet interrupted. "Look, you've got to come up with a better lie than that."

Ada's eyes burned, as well as her face. "I've never told a lie in my life, and now suddenly nobody ever believes me!"

"Okay, okay! I'm sorry." Violet made a helpless motion with her arms. "But if that's the truth you'll have to start telling lies before they put you in the looney bin."

Ada sniffed. She wasn't going to cry. She wasn't. "You keep saying it's not your business."

Violet shrugged and stood. "There's the bus."

The bus was too noisy for talk, so they looked at some gaudy magazines Violet had brought on the ride. At the school, Ada spent most of the day sitting in the office, when she was not being shuffled to a nurse to be pricked by needles, or to another office to fill out forms with information that was not believed. She received texts on unfamiliar subjects, and was asked how far she had advanced in them, and took a test that seemed to cover all subjects at once. By the time she went out to the bus she was worn out.

When she saw Violet on the stairs, she threw her arms about her. "I'm so glad to see you!" she said. "This is the most dreadful day I've ever suffered in my life!"

"We should all have it so good," responded Violet, coldly.

The degree to which Ada felt the rebuff must have shown on her face, for Violet immediately softened. "Sorry. I've gone through that paperwork crud so often it don't seem like much to me. Come on, or we'll miss our seat." On the bus, Violet settled herself by the window and pulled out her magazines. "Want one?"

"No thank you," said Ada, opening her Texas history book. She had begun reading it during the day; but it was not as easy piecing together the history of the past hundred years as it should have been. The book referred casually to things like "World War I" and the "Great Depression," as if everyone were already supposed to know about these things.

Ada resumed reading after supper. The shelter's schedule required its inmates to retire to their rooms for an hour on weeknights, so Violet sat at the metal shelf serving as a desk, working at arithmetic, while Ada sat on the bed and tried to puzzle out what had turned her old world into her present one. After a time she tossed down the book with an irritated sigh.

"S'matter?" asked Violet.

"I don't see why I should tell you," said Ada. "You'll only call me a liar again."

Violet rubbed something out with the pink stuff at the end of the pencil. "You any good at figuring out when cars are going to pass each other and how many apples you can buy and stuff?"

"Passably," said Ada.

"Tell you what. You help me figure out these word problems, and I won't call you a liar, whatever I think."

Ada flopped back on the bed in an unladylike manner. It was as good an offer as she was likely to get. "The book on Texas history leaves out a great deal that I want to know. For instance: In the last chapter, it describes how Houston was selected as the command base for the space program. But it doesn't say when we met the Klingons."

Violet's pencil stopped moving. "Why should there be anything about Klingons in a history book?"

"I'd think meeting folks from a different planet would be more important to talk about than—than anything that's in here!"

Violet stared. "That 'Star Trek' show—it's all made-up."

"I realize that," said Ada, impatiently. "I'm not stupid, whatever you may think. But the Klingon and the—the Ferengi had to come from somewhere. Photographs don't lie."

Violet looked at her a long time before answering. "You really don't know, do you?"

"I wouldn't ask you if I did!" Ada's voice slid up the scale and she began to tremble.

"Hey, it's okay." Violet got up and opened a bureau drawer full of magazines. "All the aliens, they come out of the makeup department. Here . . . see . . ." She brought one of her magazines to the bed, pointing to a series of pictures. "This shows you. They take Michael Dorn—that's the actor that plays Worf the Klingon—and they put all this gunk on him."

Ada studied the photographs, the discomfort in her throat loosening. She never would have believed that the knobby-headed character on the show could be such an ordinary-looking man, but the pictures showed clearly how it had been accomplished. She began to laugh. "N-no wonder you thought I was stupid!"

"What year did you say you were from?" asked Violet.

"Eighteen and ninety-one," sniffed Ada. She seemed to be crying as much as laughing. "May I borrow a handkerchief?"

Violet tore a thin, soft sheet of paper out of a box on the nightstand. "So you don't know about Kleenex, neither?"

Ada shook her head. By the time she finished wiping her face and blowing her nose, the Kleenex was a crumpled ball. "I don't know about Kleenex, or cars, or TV, or—or Ninja Turtles. It's interesting, but I wish I could go home."

"Okay," said Violet. "So you're from a hundred years ago. A hundred years ago black people had to ride on the back of the bus and white people did all they could to keep us down. So why weren't you mad when they stuck you in the same room as me?"

"It's not like that!" Ada protested—against a twinge of conscience. "I'm not allowed to play with—with girls like you, but they ride on the streetcars same as anyone. And when President Harrison came, Ma—someone I know complained because there were black people in line ahead of her to shake his hand."

Violet drew up her knees, regarding Ada quizzically. "So tell me again, how'd you get here?"

Patiently, Ada went through it all again. Violet flopped back on the pillows and chewed her nails. "I tell you what," she said, "I'm not sure I believe you, but I am sure you're not a liar. You believe this like I believe my name is Violet. Anybody talks to you long enough is going to figure that out."

"Good," said Ada.

Violet shook her head and thumped the pillow. "Bad! 'Cause no social worker's going to believe some sugarplum fairy sent you forward in time! If you don't come up with a good story, you're going to get placed in the mental health system, and sister, once you're in that rat race, you'll never get out!"

She said this so fiercely that Ada felt cold. "But what can I do?" she asked, meekly.

"Two things." Violet jumped up and began pacing the room. "First, we got to find that well and make another wish, see if the fairy'll come through for you. That'd be the best thing."

"And second?"

"Second, I help you make up something the social workers'll buy. I can do it, too." Violet grinned. "I'm a pro." She plopped back into the chair in front of her arithmetic. "So, you going to help me with these stupid word problems now?"

"That was the bargain," said Ada, feeling as if a burden had been lifted from her heart.

CHAPTER SIX

The Orphanage

Mr. Bauer drove Amber to the orphanage in a buggy. "I wish I knew some other place to send you," he said after they'd crossed the river.

"I know," said Amber. "It was nice of you to let me sleep at your house last night." Even through the numb shock of her wish's failure, she had been impressed with the Bauer family's kindness to a total stranger, at a time when they had their own troubles. "I hope Ada turns up real soon."

Mr. Bauer sighed. "She is not a bad girl, our Ada," he said, "but she is too independent. I fear she has done something foolish; but perhaps she will return sadder and wiser today."

Amber wondered what her own mom and dad were saying, a hundred years from now.

"What's the orphanage like?" she asked.

Mr. Bauer shrugged. "Mrs. Bauer is on the committee. They will train you to keep house and be useful in society." He watched the horse's reddish brown ears glumly for a minute, then brightened. "But you will not be there long. You are my Ada's age, I think—almost thirteen? Orphans are let out on their own when they reach fourteen."

Amber decided to stop asking questions and enjoy the scenery. Most of the houses were prettier than the cracker-box-shaped ones of her own neighborhood; but some were surprisingly small. Pavement was rare, so the air was full of dust that coated her glasses. Even at the slow rate at which the horse trotted, they left town much too soon—and outside of town was nothing but flat ground covered with grass and flowers.

Amber saw the orphanage some time before they reached it—a house as gray and ugly as anything could be that wasn't made of concrete. Other buildings stood around at random—barn, chicken house, hog pen, and so on. It smelled fairly icky. Apart from some big boys and a couple of men with hoes in between the rows of crops, nobody was in sight.

Mr. Bauer rang an iron bell next to the door, while Amber craned her neck trying to see in one of the windows. There were way too many windows, all open, all with paper blinds. Anybody could be behind those blinds. Dracula. Freddy Krueger. Drug pushers that crept up on you in your sleep and injected you with morphine so that you woke up an addict—

A short thin girl in a tall wide apron opened the door. "May I speak to Mrs. MacRae?" asked Mr. Bauer, removing his hat.

She bobbed briefly. "This way, please," she said, without interest. Amber followed, scolding herself. Drug pushers and child murderers hadn't been invented yet; and there weren't any such things as vampires. Or if there were, they wouldn't hang out in orphanages. Amber didn't have anything to be afraid of.

All the same, she didn't like the looks of Mrs. MacRae. Her hair was pulled tight, her black dress covered her from her chin down, and a ring of keys at her belt clanked when she moved. She looked at Amber as if she thought she might be carrying a switchblade.

Amber stood with her hands behind her back and her feet together, letting Mr. Bauer repeat the lie she had told last night about her parents having died of consumption.

"This isn't a consumptive home," said Mrs. MacRae, taking Amber under the chin and turning her face side to side. "If you're diseased, child, we must send you someplace else."

Amber had picked consumption because a lot of people died of it in old-fashioned books. She didn't have any good idea of what it was. "I'm fine," she said, pulling away from the woman's hands. "It was just my folks."

Mrs. MacRae's eyebrows drew together. "What is your name?"

"Amber Burak."

"Amber Burak, what?"

"Just Amber Burak."

"Don't you mean, Amber Burak, ma'am?"

"Oh." She would have to remember to talk like a book. "Yes, ma'am. I'm sorry."

"And did your parents raise you to be a good Christian?"

Dad was Jewish, when he was anything; and Mom had no religion. Would people a hundred years ago be prejudiced against Jews? Bauer was a German name—Amber had a vivid memory of all the stories her grandfather had told her about Germans. But they'd catch her in the lie if she claimed to be a Christian. "Um . . . no, ma'am."

Mrs. MacRae frowned. "We will have to instruct you, then. And will you undertake to work hard at the lessons and the housework we give you, and be a good and obedient girl?"

"Yes, ma'am." Like she had a choice.

Mrs. MacRae opened the door and called down the hall, where the girl in the apron was sweeping. "Ethel! Amber will be staying with us. Take her to find some decent clothing."

Amber, remembering to act like a girl in a book, bobbed good-bye awkwardly to Mr. Bauer. "I hope Ada's waiting for you when you get home," she said. "Thanks a lot. Sir."

He smiled a small, kind smile underneath his mustache. Ethel led the way up a flight of bare stairs where her shoes clattered, but Amber's only squeaked. Ethel looked down. "I never saw shoes like that before."

"Neither did I," said Amber, who had spent most of a sleepless night thinking up good lies. "I found them in somebody's garbage."

They went down a long hall, and Ethel pointed into a long room. Windows ran all the way down one side, and beds all the way down both. "That's where we sleep," said Ethel. "You hang your clothes on a hook by your bed and put your shoes side by side at the foot. And when the bell rings in the morning, you line up at the washstand according to age and wash your face and ears. Pushing in line or not washing or letting your clothes fall on the floor is all worth one switch."

"One what?" Amber, who had slowed down to look at the room, hurried a couple of steps to catch up.

"One switch," repeated Ethel. "Miss Devine keeps a peach switch locked in the cupboard."

Amber stopped dead. "You mean—if you break a rule here, they hit you with a piece of wood?"

Ethel turned around. "Well—of course."

Amber opened her mouth and shut it again. All the words in her head seemed to have frozen up.

"If you're real bad they lock you in the cupboard," continued Ethel. "It's mostly boys that are that bad, though. And nobody ever gets more than ten switches. That's if you steal something." Seeing that Amber didn't move, Ethel made a vague motion with her head and one hand. "Come along. The clothes cupboard is at the end of the hall by the nursery. I'll have to get Mrs. Prine to open it."

Amber made her feet move again and followed her to a big piece of furniture beside a closed door, at which Ethel knocked. From inside came various small sounds, which got louder as the door opened; but Amber couldn't see inside, because the fat woman filled up the opening. Ethel made one of her bobs, and Amber copied her. "What is it?" demanded the fat woman, fat yellow curls quivering around her face.

"Please, ma'am, there's a new girl, and Mrs. MacRae says to get her decently dressed."

The woman's piggy eyes widened when they looked at Amber. "Glory be, but she needs it!" She stepped out, closing the door behind her before Amber got more than a glimpse of a row of cribs and some discouraged-looking small children doing nothing in particular.

"That brother of yours is a peck of trouble," Mrs. Prine

grumbled, fiddling with the keys at her waist—big, spiky things that could have been used as weapons if she had been mugged. "I swan he don't belong here one bit. We'll have to send him to the home for the feebleminded one of these days, and you'd best make up your mind to it." She jabbed a key into the door of the clothes cupboard.

Ethel looked the faintest shade paler. "Wh-what's he done today, ma'am?"

"Same as he does every day." Mrs. Prine jerked open the door, revealing shelves stacked with folded clothes and sheets. She cast an eye over Amber and began jerking items off the tops of stacks. "I must've told him three times to keep away from that window, and he stares out like he never heard. Luella's had to box his ears twice, and I've slapped him upside the head once my own self." She thrust a pile into Amber's hands. "There. What's your name, child?"

"Amber Burak, ma'am," said Amber, remembering to bob but not doing it well because she was afraid of dropping her clothes.

"Amber Burak! What kind of name is that? You must be some kind of a foreigner."

Amber had been halfway mad, watching Ethel's face while Mrs. Prine ran down her brother; and the nasty emphasis on *foreigner* finished the job. "I was born in San Antonio," she said, "but my grandad barely came out of Poland alive. And we're proud of him."

Mrs. Prine slapped her, so quickly and so casually that Amber could not respond. She was still realizing that it had happened when Mrs. Prine put the keys back on her belt and said, calmly: "You watch that mouth of yours,

64

Miss Amber Burak." She was back inside the nursery before Amber could form a reply.

She followed Ethel back to the dorm room, seething. "She didn't have any right to do that," she said. "It's no business of hers where I'm from. I should've told her—"

"Hush!" Ethel looked up and down the hall as if expecting Mrs. Prine to pounce from hiding, although there was nothing whatever to hide behind. "You'll get in trouble."

"I don't care. I'll get her in trouble right back."

"You can't." Ethel twisted her right hand inside of her left. Was that what books called "wringing your hands"? "There's no one for you to get her in trouble with."

"Bull," said Amber stoutly. She laid down her stack of clothes on a bed. "Where's the bathroom? I'm totally grungy."

"Grungy?" repeated Ethel. "Is that a Polish word?"

"Uh . . . yeah—I mean yes. For dirty. Could I get a bath?"

"Not in the middle of the day!" Ethel sounded as if she'd asked for the moon and a side order of stars. "We have baths every Saturday, so you'll be able to wash tonight."

Amber was dimly aware that people had used to only bathe once a week, but she hadn't considered how that would apply to her here and now. Gross. She reached around the back of her neck and fiddled with the buttons of the yellow dress, which she'd had to put back on after Mr. Bauer found her. "What happens to my stuff?"

"It'll go down to the laundry," said Ethel. "What's worth fixing goes to the help and the rest is burned."

"So we can't keep anything?"

Ethel shook her head. "What's that there?"

"My purse. I'd hate to lose it." The sundress she could live without, but the purse had her money, comb, and atomic fireballs. She snapped it open. "You like cinnamon candy?"

"Candy?" Ethel perked up.

Amber handed her one, and she puzzled over the wrapping. Amber took one too, popping it through the seam on the end and into her mouth. Ethel copied her, making a sharp sound as the cinnamon hit her tongue. "Where'd you get this?" she mumbled.

"It's a secret," said Amber. "Are there any good hiding places around here?"

Ethel, her mouth too occupied with the fireball to speak, beckoned her to the stove, a black round thing on stumpy legs. Ethel pushed the door to the room shut, got down on her hands and knees, and counted floorboards from the wall, then pressed down on a join. The other end rose, and Amber could see where people had stuck things under the floor—matches, a coverless book, a string of beads, a one-armed cloth doll with a china head. "It'll be safe here," Ethel said, "honor bright."

"Excellent!" Amber started lowering in the purse. "Would your little brother like a fireball? Or maybe some gum?"

"He'd only get caught," she said, "but thank you for asking. I don't—he doesn't—thank you."

The atomic fireball seemed to have enchanted Ethel, and she said nothing about how slow Amber was at getting dressed in the orphan uniform. The pants, or drawers, pulled tight with a drawstring; then stockings went all the way up her legs and fastened to the drawers with buttons; then there was a full white slip—what Ethel called a chemise—then a blue-checked dress like a knee-length, long-sleeved sack, and finally an apron, called a pinafore, like the one Ethel wore. The shoes were the worst—high and tight, with lots of buttons too small for her fingers to handle. Ethel brought her a hook for catching them and pulling them through the buttonholes, which helped some.

Although the day was not especially warm and all the windows were open, all those clothes plus the effort of getting the shoes on made Amber sweat. "I don't think these shoes are the right size," she complained, flopping back onto a bed.

"She gave you the biggest we had," said Ethel. "Now we only need to braid your hair, and you'll be fit for anyone to see."

"I don't think I looked so bad before." Amber tried to make two neat, even braids; but her hair seemed fatter on one side than the other. She wound up letting Ethel do the job for her. She pulled Amber's hair so tight it was hard to blink; but the back of her neck was cooler.

"Where is everybody?" Amber asked. "There's a couple dozen beds here, but the only big kid I've seen is you."

"Everybody's doing their Saturday jobs. Which I've got to go back and finish mine before lunch, or I won't get none."

"I'll help you," said Amber.

This was easy to offer, but turned out to be hard to do. In addition to the sweeping, the doorknobs had to be polished; and a more pointless, finicky job Amber had never tried to do. She met several other girls during the process, all working. It seemed a waste of time to Amber, a lot of waxing and polishing of things that were already shiny and clean.

She was glad when a gong rang with a deep, booming clang and Ethel said: "Lunch! Come along; they dock you if you're late."

Not anxious to learn what "docking" was, Amber followed Ethel to a long trough in the backyard, where girls and boys lined up to wash their hands. The boys wore baggy gray pants and blue-checked shirts. Something was funny about this place—boys, girls, everybody.

While she stood at a long table waiting for Mrs. MacRae to say grace, Amber realized that not only did all the kids wear the same clothes and have the same hairstyles, but they all had the same expressions on their faces. And their faces were all the same color. No Mexicans, no blacks, no Asians; not even any suntans.

The sameness did not quite extend to the grown-ups. Mrs. Prine at the foot of the table was fat and blond, as opposed to Mrs. MacRae—skinny, dark, and plain—at the head. At the other table was a woman with gray hair and a mouth like a trap, and a gray man whose mouth was almost hidden by his mustache. All the women wore black; the man wore overalls.

Out of fifty kids, not one looked up or spoke as they shoveled down their food. One of the girls had a crutch propped next to her, and one of the boys ate awkwardly due to the twisted shape of his upper lip. No glasses, apart from her own, or even any left-handed people. The spoons rose and fell on the right side of each shallow bowl, as if the children were wind-up mannequins in a store window.

Creepy, thought Amber. If I stay here a whole year, will I look like that?

No. Absolutely not! Amber longed to run off by herself to try to work out a plan; but immediately after lunch she and the other big girls were herded off to a room on the top floor, where they sat on hard chairs and sewed sheets while the steel-trap woman—Miss Devine—read aloud from a little brown book.

Amber had never sewed before. It didn't look hard, but she and Ethel were both working on the same sheet at once, and it seemed like every time she stuck the needle in, Ethel tugged the cloth and the needle went someplace she didn't mean it to. Then she'd try to stick it up again from the bottom, and it never came out where she expected. Plus the story was totally boring, all about some kid resisting temptation.

When Amber raised her eyes she could see, through the row of windows, the boys in the fields, and carts and buggies creeping along the road. From up here she could see where the hills started, and trees that were probably on the river.

Ethel kicked her ankle softly. Amber turned crossly and opened her mouth, but Ethel held up her finger and motioned frantically toward the steel-trap lady. Amber bent her head over the sheet and watched out of the corners of her eyes. Miss Devine would read a line or two, then look up suddenly. The girls seemed to have the timing on this down. One of the big girls kept pointing at Amber's sheet, smirking; but she always had her head bent over her own work when Miss Devine looked up. Annoyed, Amber turned a cold stare on her. The girl sat up straight and pretended she'd never been looking in that direction.

"If you are quite done with admiring Jane Henderson, perhaps you will favor us by continuing your share of the task, Amber," said Miss Devine, breaking into the drone of the story sharply.

Rats! She'd been so busy turning on her stare she'd forgotten to watch out. "I'm sorry, ma'am," Amber said. "Her hair looks so pretty I couldn't look away." She could tell Jane Henderson was dying to make a face at her for that remark (for nobody could have pretty hair under the circumstances; and Jane's was the color of dirty dishwater). Amber pretended to be busy with the sheet, and waited for the story to start up again.

Instead, Miss Devine stood. "Do you think we don't pay attention to our children because there are so many of them?" Her dress rustled across the floor. "I want you to understand something, miss. Because we have so many children, we can't afford not to pay attention to what each and every one is doing." She stood directly over Amber. "You call that a seam? Pick every last stitch out, and redo them properly."

Amber pushed her glasses up her nose. "I'll try. Ma'am. I never did this before."

"If you've been raised in idleness, you'll find that things are different here," said Miss Devine.

Didn't these people have anything better to do than pick on her? "Lots of girls can't sew by the time they're twelve."

Miss Devine slapped her, exactly as Mrs. Prine had done earlier. "Hey!" cried Amber; but Miss Devine was not listening.

"We don't tolerate back talk here. You pick out all those stitches, and you won't go down to supper till they're done right. And if I hear one more word out of you, you won't have any supper at all. Do you understand?"

Amber opened her mouth to say "You can't do that!", shut it again, and nodded. She didn't know what institutional caregivers couldn't do in 1891. She did know that Mom was always complaining about the things they got away with in 1991. Probably whatever Miss Devine and Mrs. Prine said they had to do to keep the kids in line, Mrs. MacRae would let them do.

Miss Devine returned to her chair and resumed reading. Ethel passed Amber a pointed metal thing and looked sympathetic. Amber smiled back grimly and took it. Probably this was to rip out the stitches with. Well, if she stayed here very long, she'd rip out more than stitches. These dudes didn't know what they'd got into when they got Amber Burak in their orphanage!

This resolution upheld her as she sewed and ripped out, sewed and ripped out, the same set of stitches over and over. When the gong rang for supper the piece was so grubby and wrinkled she could have picked out the part she'd been working on from across the room. She was hungry, and tired, and crabby, and hot, and her jaws ached from saying nothing.

All the girls and Miss Devine stood up when the gong rang. Miss Devine rustled over to look at Amber's sewing. "I see you're finally getting your stitches to be a decent size," she said. "Stay here and finish."

"Don't I get supper?" asked Amber, as calmly as she could.

"Don't take that tone," said Miss Devine. "If you're done when I return there'll be no difficulty about your eating."

Some of the girls looked at her sympathetically, some meanly, and some not at all, as they filed out. The door shut behind them, and Amber saw and heard the key in the lock.

Amber wanted to scream. Instead she bunched up the sheet, threw it on the floor, and kicked the wall till her toes hurt. Then she picked up the book, which Miss Devine had left on the table, and threw it at the wall. She wrote every bad word she knew, English and Spanish, on the blackboard at one end of the room; and drew a picture of Miss Devine, at which she hurled the book until she felt better. Then she erased everything, picked up the sheet, and took it to a chair by a window.

She squinted, and tugged, and checked each individual stitch before she went on to the next one, finally getting a straight, tight row of them connected to the part Ethel had worked on. By that time the light was almost gone, and she figured Miss Devine would be coming to unlock her soon. One ear open for sounds in the hall, she carefully placed a dozen pins in the thin cushion of Miss Devine's chair. She hoped this would work. Miss Devine had so much underwear under that noisy skirt that the back stuck out at least six inches from her behind.

Old-timey shoes on bare floors made a good early-warning system. Amber was by the window pretending to sew when Miss Devine returned. She said "yes, ma'am" and "no, ma'am" and was humble enough to gag a maggot. Miss Devine seemed pleased.

Supper, cold, consisted mostly of plain corn bread and oversalted ham. Amber had been unable to drink all her milk at lunch because it had been warm and watery; tonight's milk had the same faults, but there wasn't enough of it to deal with the salt. Alone in the dim hall, hearing the other children outside playing quietly, Amber's anger faded. She was too tired for it.

Her back ached. Her head ached. Her feet and fingers and even the backs of her ears were sore. Sweat made her nose so slick her glasses wouldn't stay up. Flies kept buzzing into her face. This wasn't what she'd wanted when she made that wish!

Amber crumbled corn bread between her fingers. Mom and Dad would be frantic, thinking about the two girls who'd been kidnapped and killed last year. She realized that if she sat here much longer she would cry. She piled her cup and silverware onto her plate and took them toward the sound of dish washing.

The kitchen was small, hot, and so dark that Amber couldn't make out the color of the clothes on the woman washing dishes. "Excuse me, ma'am," said Amber, "where do I scrape my plate?"

The woman turned around. "Who you talking to?"

"You, ma'am." Amber remembered to bob.

"None of your sass." She pointed at a bucket, where flies clustered thick and disgusting. "There's the pig bucket. The way you children eat, that poor pig's like to starve to death."

Amber walked a little harder than she needed to on the way to the pig bucket. "Doesn't anybody in this place have anything better to do than tell me how to talk?" she demanded before she could stop herself. "I'm not being sassy. I said 'excuse me' and 'ma'am' and I even bobbed! So what do you people want, anyway?"

The woman laughed out loud. Amber finished scraping the plate. "What's so funny?"

The woman wiped her forehead with a corner of her apron. "Child, you're having a terrible day, ain't you? Who was it told you you had to curtsy and say 'ma'am' to the old colored cook?"

"Nobody," said Amber. "Why shouldn't I? You're as grown-up as anybody, aren't you?"

"I reckon so; but I'm nowhere near as white."

"What difference does that make?" When the cook started laughing again, she remembered. A hundred years ago, what color you were made a big difference.

"What's your name, child?"

"Amber Burak," said Amber. "What's yours?"

"Sally Manger Ford. Everybody calls me Aunt Sally Manger, and you better, too."

Amber was finding it hard to talk with all that salt still on her tongue. "Can—may I have a drink of water? Please?"

Aunt Sally Manger nodded toward a pump mounted in the wall. Amber's first try at filling her cup got water all over her—which was okay, as hot as it was in here. She drank three cups in a row, thinking: This poor woman is washing dishes for the whole orphanage all by herself, without a dishwasher. Amber wasn't sure she could face all those children right now. "I don't feel like playing," she said, unfastening the buttons at her wrists so she could roll up her sleeves. "I'll help you with the dishes."

Aunt Sally Manger objected; but Amber started washing and by the time the gong rang again, she knew that Aunt Sally Manger had six children and a husband, and the husband worked for the orphanage, too, as a handyman. Amber went over her story about her parents dying of consumption; and Aunt Sally Manger told her about some of her fellow orphans. "You watch out for that Jane Henderson," she said, "she carries tales. And her brother ain't no better. Mr. Huff says boys will be boys, but what I say—there's the gong for prayers. You go long now."

For prayers, everybody knelt on the dining room benches and folded their hands while Mrs. MacRae stood at the head of the room, read a chapter from the Bible, and then said the prayer for them. The Bible bit was about King Solomon building a temple. Amber didn't see what it had to do with anything. The prayer was about God making the children grateful for all that the good Christian people of San Antonio were doing for them.

After prayers they all went to a washhouse, a big wooden shed full of steam and tubs. Amber scrubbed herself as clean as she could in the tiny tub of scalding water, with soap that wouldn't lather, as her glasses fogged up. Miss Devine shoved a scratchy white nightgown at her, and she followed the other girls up to the dorm, where she got the bed next to Ethel's after a little negotiating with the former occupant.

Looking very impressed with her own importance, Jane Henderson saw the other girls into bed, then blew out the single candle. "How do you ever get to use the stuff under the stove with that witch in the room?" Amber whispered to Ethel.

"Oh, the book's hers." Ethel yawned. "She don't mind broken rules, as long as she's the one breaking them. Good night, Amber."

"Good night, Ethel."

"Y'all be quiet down there," said Jane Henderson.

CHAPTER SEVEN

Escape Plans

By Saturday Ada was exhausted by the twentieth century and would gladly have signed up for a lifetime of looking after her little brother and sisters, if only she could see them again.

She began attending school full-time on Wednesday, after spending most of Tuesday waiting in a cold office for immunization shots. Children overflowed the school's original building, so classes had to be held in subsidiary buildings on the grounds. These children and the ones at the shelter made fun of her shoes, her mode of speech, and her name; called her a show-off in English class and a moron in science and history; asked her questions whose terms she could not understand and declared her stuck-up when she could not answer.

What she would have done without Violet, Ada could not imagine. Her roommate may have believed she was insane, but at least she believed politely. She wanted to know all about Ada's family, and school, and what black people she had known in 1891. In return Violet told Ada the meanings of words like *teenage*, *mutant*, and *ninja*; the identities of people like "The New Kids on the Block"; how to neatly eat spaghetti; and how to tie the tennis shoes that were found for her in the Goodwill box.

Unfortunately, Violet was not always around when needed. Separate teachers were in charge of different subjects for each grade, and these subjects were further subdivided according to ability, so no two people ever shared classes all day. When she and Violet were in the same room, they sat next to each other in the back, Violet cuing her about how she should act. When alone, Ada struggled along as best she could. So many things had changed, she could barely write a word with confidence anymore.

"The English teacher loves you," Violet assured Ada in the bathroom on Saturday morning when Ada was fretting about the composition she had written on Friday. "I bet she never had a kid that could use *mellifluous* in a sentence before."

"But the essay was such a mess!" said Ada. "I've never in my life used so much paper. We always worked out our compositions on a slate first and then copied it fair onto paper." She squeezed toothpaste onto her toothbrush—a process that resulted, every day, in having to clean a dollop out of the sink. What ever happened to tooth powder? she wondered crossly.

"Never mind," said Violet. "You may not be here to find out what your grade is."

"Why not?" Ada paused with her hand on the cold-water tap.

"Because we're going to find your well today and see if the sugarplum fairy'll take you back," said Violet.

"How? I didn't think we could leave the shelter."

"Sure we can! Only most people don't have any place to go, and we've got to check in with Loyce and it's not worth it." Violet snapped an elastic band around one of her braids. "You remember Ms. Burak's kid disappeared?"

Ada nodded around her toothbrush.

"They're going to search, like for Heidi—you don't know who that is. A girl named Heidi disappeared last year and a bunch of folks got together and had house-to-house searches, knocking on doors all over town carrying her picture."

Ada rinsed her mouth. "Did they find her?"

"Yeah. She was dead. So they set up a foundation named after her; and the Buraks went to it for help, and there's going to be a search. And we're going to volunteer."

"Of course I'll be happy to help, but I don't see how that gets me back to the Haunted Lot."

Violet fastened her last braid and grinned. "See, she disappeared from this place called the Streicher Children's Center. I stayed there awhile last fall. And right next to it, there's this empty space that the kids call the Haunted Lot. People go there to smoke dope."

Ada gaped. "But—the Streicher Children's Center? The Streichers were our neighbors!"

Violet nodded as impatient knocks began on the bathroom door. "Anyway, Loyce'll ask for volunteers to help with the house-to-house in that area this morning. We really will search, too. I don't know Amber except to look at, but Ms. Burak's the nicest social worker I've had."

"I wonder what Mamma and Pappa think has become of me," said Ada, quietly, on their way downstairs.

"They'll be worried, but it shouldn't be that bad," said Violet. "Y'all didn't have sex maniacs and dope pushers and child murderers back then."

"I don't know what a sex maniac or a dope pusher is," said Ada, "but people do murder children. Or they fall in the ditch and drown, though I'm a little old to do that. And I'm old enough for the white slavers to pick up. As far as they know, I could be in Chicago or—or China in a den of vice right now."

"What's a white slaver?"

Cold cereal for breakfast again this morning. Ada, who had not particularly liked anything she had eaten at the shelter, took a box at random, wondering how to explain a term which had never been explained to her with any precision. "They kidnap women and make them drunk— or feed them opium, if the kidnappers are Chinese—and make them live, ah, immoral lives."

"They do, huh?" Violet selected Rice Krispies. "Opium is what they make heroin out of, isn't it?"

"It doesn't make heroines out of these women," said Ada. "I just told you, the slavers make them lead immoral lives."

"No, no, heroin. Dope." Violet sat down and tore open her milk carton, looking thoughtful. "So I guess you did have pushers in those days. I didn't know that." She brightened. "Anyway, maybe your folks won't have time to worry. Maybe you'll come back to the same time you left."

"Why should I?"

"Why shouldn't you? You can make any wish you want."

This was both true and comforting. Ada felt quite hopeful when Loyce came in and announced the search, and she and Violet leaped to volunteer.

Only the older children went, piling into the back of a car called Loyce's station wagon. Ada watched the world zip by from on top of the highway with great interest. When she recognized the Streichers' familiar roof rising at an unfamiliar angle and with unexpected closeness, she grabbed Violet's hand and squeezed it. "That's it," she said.

"The Streicher Children's Center," said Violet.

Ada turned inside her seat belt to keep it in sight, but they were already descending the off ramp. "The way home," she said.

Ada had a bad moment when they were told they'd be assigned an adult to search with, but Violet reassured her as they sat on the curb. "We'll be in groups, so she'll have other kids to keep track of. It's just so we don't wind up missing, too. We'll be able to slip off without any problem."

"But—if it works, I will wind up missing," Ada protested.

Violet shrugged. "So? Tell you what—if you vanish, I'll vanish, too. I'm good at it. I can turn up in time for school, and I'll have thought up a good lie about how you went home."

"I wish you weren't so interested in telling lies."

"Hey. A gal's got to do what a gal's got to do."

Ada felt she should say more, but she didn't believe Violet would listen. Instead she studied the photograph of Amber. In some ways, she resembled Ada—same color hair and eyes, a similarity of complexion—but Amber had spectacles and a broad nose, lightly dusted with freckles. "Wouldn't it be tidy, if Amber were found the same day I disappear here?" she said. "I appeared the same day she vanished."

"That'd be good," said Violet. "I'll stick around if that happens. There'd be a big news story, and—what's wrong?"

"I just remembered." Ada sat up, trying to get her skirt to cover her knees. "The reason I didn't go back to the well that first night was that I didn't have anything to toss into it. The—thingamabob—doesn't like money."

"No sweat. I know where to get some candy."

"I haven't any money I can spend."

"So? I've got some. I try to keep it for emergencies, like when I have to vanish."

"Why should you have to vanish?" asked Ada.

Violet's face shut, like a window with the blinds pulled.

Ada and Violet found themselves in a group headed by Mrs. Burak herself. She looked even more tired and harried than she had the first time Ada had seen her, but she smiled bravely, greeting each child by name. "It's good of y'all to help," she said. "And don't be afraid to tell me anything you find. It's a terrible thing not to know where someone is; worse even than knowing that they're dead." She looked hard at Violet.

"Yes, ma'am," said Violet.

They walked to their assigned street in straggling single file, Mrs. Burak moving to talk to each of the children in turn. When she spoke to Ada she apologized for not coming to see her. "I usually follow up better on the children I place," she said. "My work has been—neglected—the last week."

"I should think so!" said Ada. "It's all right, ma'am. Violet has been looking after me."

"You and she have something in common, you know." Mrs. Burak watched Violet's braids, quivering as she strode along. They were passing a park where a few children clambered on play equipment, and a number of grown men idled on benches.

"What's that, ma'am?"

"Neither of you tells a satisfactory story," said Mrs. Burak. "Or—that's not quite true. Violet has far too many satisfactory stories. I've placed her six times since last year. Each time she had a different story, and a different name."

Ada considered this. It did not particularly surprise her.

"And then there's you. Ada Bauer from 1891." Mrs. Burak wiped perspiration from her forehead. "Believe me, I understand the impulse. All these folks are poking into your personal business, asking questions that maybe hurt to answer; and even if you answer, maybe their meddling will make it worse. Vi thinks she has the system pegged, but systems are made of people. And people don't like to be laughed at."

"No, ma'am." Ada sorted through the things she could say. "Violet says, if I hold to my first story, I'll be sent to a home for the insane."

"I wouldn't place you there, if I could help it," said Mrs. Burak. "But if Dr. Cunningham tells the judge you're delusional, it won't be my decision."

Ada felt cold. *I don't have to worry about it,* she reminded herself.

The neighborhood they searched was some distance from Ada's. With all of her familiar landmarks gone, she could not tell how distant—perhaps all the way into what had been "the colored part of town." If so, it had improved, the one- and two-room houses replaced by frame cottages. She missed the china trees, and it seemed strange that streets so quiet should be paved.

At first she was nervous, knocking on strange doors, but she and Violet did the first few together, and after that it grew easier. Ada gave out copies of the picture and of a phone number to be called, answering the same questions over and over.

"Hey, Ms. Burak!" called Violet as they completed a section of street. "Can we stop at this icehouse? I've got a dollar!"

"Hang onto it, then," said Mrs. Burak. "I'll buy us all drinks and ask the cashier to put up a poster."

The icehouse was a windowless building, with a huge metal bin outside labeled ICE. Inside, racks of shelves held bread, canned goods, cleaning products, and an assortment of bright packages that Ada realized, from the smell, were candy. Violet waved her hand. "What you think the sugarplum fairy'll like?"

"I don't even know what's in these," said Ada, picking up a bright orange package.

"Chocolate, mostly. That's a Reese's peanut butter cup."

Ada, who had tasted peanut butter once, made a face and laid it down again. "Is there any *peloncillo*? I know it likes that."

"I never even heard of *peloncillo* till you told me about it. We'd better not take anything that'll melt, so that lets out all the chocolate."

By the time Mrs. Burak had purchased Cokes and finished talking to the clerk, they had settled on caramels, which would melt slowly and were, by modern standards, cheap. After tossing one in the well, Violet would still have half a dozen to repay her investment. It was hard for Ada to go back to knocking on doors, knowing that her return home was imminent.

Finally, they returned to the Streicher house for lunch. The searchers picnicked on sandwiches, hot dogs, and Saratoga (now called potato) chips. The highway had been built over the place where the carriage house should be; the smooth lawn had been turned into a playground; and Mrs. Streicher's rose beds had been covered up by pavement and cars. The china trees were replaced by a couple of pecans, bound with huge yellow ribbons. Ada tried not to think about what had happened to her own house.

"What truly bothers me," said Mrs. Burak to Loyce, "is that when they searched this lot over here, they found an open well."

"It's criminal that it's there," said Mr. Burak, on the other side of her. "No cover over it, nothing. It's not on the City Water Board maps."

"You don't think she fell in, do you?" asked Loyce.

Mrs. Burak shook her head. "We were able to lower a man in, and there's nothing but junk."

"There's water in the bottom though," said Mr. Burak.

"Bodies float," said Mrs. Burak, her voice shrill.

Ada scooted back her chair. "May I be excused, please?"

"Sure, Ada," said Loyce, falsely cheerful. "Don't go far."

"I'll go with you," said Violet.

They went into the house first, through the back door. Ada had often been in this kitchen, when Pinkie or Billy was wheedling cookies out of Mary Reba. Only the windows looked the same. The cook was a Mexican, and not a good-tempered one. "You don't belong in here! Go on!"

"We're looking for the bathroom," said Violet with dignity. She started down the hall to the front door, but Ada turned.

"If we leave through the parlor, they won't be able to see us from the picnic tables."

"Which is the parlor?" asked Violet, following her. "Oh, the business offices. I never was in there."

The sight of her parlor would have made Mrs. Streicher weep. The molded ceilings were dusty, and filing cabinets, desks, and computers stood where her precious parlor suite had been. At least the door leading out onto the porch was operational, though the bower of tea roses was long gone. Ada swung over the rail and leaped wide enough to avoid landing in a flower bed that was no longer there.

"Hey, awesome!" exclaimed Violet, picking herself up from an attempt which had not gotten half as far. "I didn't know you could jump like that!"

"We used to play follow the leader," said Ada. "Billy would lead us through there, knowing we would get in trouble for smashing the flowers; so I learned to leap them, to show him."

Violet laughed. Together they climbed the fence of thick wire intertwined in a diamond pattern that had replaced the Streichers' graceful iron pickets, and circled the block, reaching the Haunted Lot unseen. The ground was still damp from the previous day's rain, and the grass and huisache had been trampled, leaving a broad path to the well. Ada hurried ahead and knelt on the edge. Violet gave her a caramel. "You've got to word this real carefully now."

"I know. I know." Ada unwrapped the plastic from the candy, thinking. "Oh, please, fairy—or whatever you are. I wish to be home in my own proper time, five minutes after I made my last wish." She dropped in the caramel.

Far below, in the unseen water, something splashed.

A mirthless giggle echoed from the depths.

The caramel shot back out and bounced off Ada's forehead.

They sat stunned. Violet recovered her powers of speech first. "What a rip!" she cried. "Hey! You!" she called down, cupping her hands around her mouth. "What's the big idea?"

There was a splashing noise, as of something swimming far below.

"Is it that you don't like caramel?" asked Ada.

Ada thought she heard the sound of something scrabbling on stone. Movement; and something new flew toward them. Both girls snatched the air, but the object fell beyond them and they scrambled after it on their hands and knees. A green hair bow.

"Oh, dear," said Ada. Amber had worn a green hair bow. They'd been describing it all morning.

Violet picked it up gingerly. "We got to tell Ms. Burak."

"Tell her what?" asked Ada. "We don't know what this means. Is Amber drowned in the well? Why didn't the diver find her, then?"

"Maybe that—whatever—kidnapped her?" Violet frowned. "Or—I don't know." She whirled and called down the well. "Come on, you! You got to tell us something better than this!"

No response. Violet took a braid in each hand and pulled. Ada had never seen her at a loss before. "At least you know I'm not insane now," she said.

"Yeah," said Violet. "For all the good that'll do!"

CHAPTER EIGHT

Ringleading

Sunday morning Miss Devine rang a bell in the doorway of the girls' dorm before the sun was up. If Ethel hadn't tugged her out of bed Amber would have gotten switched, because her first reaction was to bury her head under her pillow and go to sleep again. The Sunday uniform was black dresses and black stockings. Amber was sweating by the time she got to the dining hall for a breakfast of grits.

Then they received books and black hats, formed lines, and walked to church. Though talking was not allowed, the air was so noisy with birds and the tramp of boots that Ethel managed to point out her brother, Grof, to Amber. One of the smallest children, he trudged along with his eyes wide open. He didn't look retarded to Amber, but Ethel watched him as if she expected him to fall down every step.

The church was a square building with none of the fancy touches of churches on TV, no stained glass or carved altars. The orphanage took up the two back rows, boys on one side of the aisle, girls on the other. "Don't they ever let you sit by your brother?" Amber asked Ethel, under cover of the organ music.

Ethel shook her head. "It's unjust! I'm sure if they'd let me be with him, he'd learn to talk. The boys scare him."

Amber had never been to a church before, though she used to go to the synagogue with Dad and Grandad for major holidays. She had kind of liked that, but this service seemed to have nothing to do with her. People sang in low, slow voices, and the minister talked about evil. Amber tugged the ends of her braids and thought of all the things she needed to ask Ethel. It seemed like such a waste to sit right next to her and not be able to talk. She had started to learn American Sign Language once; maybe if she could remember the alphabet she could teach Ethel.

Eventually the congregation was invited to take communion at the altar. Amber knew it was some specifically Christian thing, so she stayed put, but most of the big girls went. Afterward, they marched back to the orphanage, arriving so hungry that Amber swallowed every bit of dry corn bread, thin soup, and blue milk.

The afternoon, to her disgust, was spent in Bible classes. Amber practiced the deaf alphabet in her lap until she was sure she had it right; and worked a loose page out of her Bible to make into a paper airplane.

This airplane not only hit the back of Miss Devine's head, but it also impressed the other kids amazingly. All the children—boys and girls—gasped and laughed as if they'd never seen such a thing before. Miss Devine was furious; but even the Hendersons primmed up their mouths and claimed to have seen nothing.

Jane Henderson came to her at the first opportunity and whispered: "What was that?"

"A paper airplane," said Amber.

"A what?"

Amber remembered that the Wright brothers hadn't flown till the twentieth century sometime. "I'm not sure I want to tell you," she said.

"If you don't, I'll say who threw it," threatened Jane.

"You do and I'll tell Miss Devine you've got a candle in your pocket," hissed Ethel.

"Girls! No gossiping!" snapped Miss Devine.

Jane Henderson smiled at her sweetly. "Amber was just asking me what a cubit was, ma'am."

"Where'd she get a candle?" Amber asked Ethel next chance she got. Miss Devine, thank goodness, could not be everywhere.

"She steals a candle from church every chance she gets," said Ethel. "She got it during communion."

Amber looked at Jane with new respect. That must have taken guts, shoplifting (churchlifting?) out in front of everybody.

Bible study lasted till suppertime, which was stringy roast beef and potatoes. Hadn't these people ever heard of vegetables? Mrs. MacRae read from the Bible and held evening prayers, though you wouldn't have thought it was necessary after all the Bible reading and praying they'd been doing all day. No bath, on a Sunday, though after sweating in that uniform Amber really wanted one; just straight up to bed, where Jane Henderson shoved a rug against the crack along the bottom of the door, stuffed her handkerchief in the keyhole, and produced her candle.

"*Lady Audley's Secret!*" whispered Luella, a girl who

90

helped Mrs. Prine with the little ones, while opening t
board under the stove.

"Not yet," said Jane Henderson, going to the foot c
Amber's bed. "How'd you do that paper airply?"

"I can't show you without paper." Amber, who had
already taken off her glasses and lain down, knelt up in
bed.

"Then show me tomorrow, or I'll tell Miss Devine."

"I'll show anybody that wants to learn"—Amber folded
her arms—"except tattletales."

"Miss Devine'll give you three switches," warned Jane.

"Let her," said Amber. "I'm not afraid of switches, and
I'm not afraid of you."

All the girls watched. In the dark, without her glasses,
they looked more alike than ever. Amber wasn't sure she
could top whatever Jane came up with to say next, so she
decided not to wait for that. She reached for her glasses.
"So what's Lady Audley's secret?"

"The book," said Ethel, hastily. "It's so sad and thrilling!
Please, Jane, read us the next chapter!"

"Very well." She turned away from Amber's bed, smiling as if she thought she had won. She lit her candle with
one of the matches from under the floorboard—striking it
on the edge of the stove, and making a sharp, blue stink—
and pulled out the coverless book. All the girls clustered
around her as the flame lit the page and her face, and she
began to read softly.

Amber sat on the foot of the bed, listening. A rustle of
rain began to fall outside. Jane read overdramatically, and
the author used such big words it was hard to figure out
what was going on. All the other girls listened with their
mouths open and their eyes wide. This isn't real, thought

Amber. Her nightgown itched the back of her neck and her mouth felt grungy.

After Jane Henderson finished one chapter she blew out the light and Luella unplugged the door and keyhole. The girls went back to bed, though it was some time before they stopped talking. "Does anybody ever get adopted out of here?" Amber asked.

"Not often," said Ethel. "Sometimes somebody from church will want a field hand or a hired girl. But they mostly take kids that are ready to go out anyway. Big girls. Like Jane." She was quiet, not quite long enough for Amber to speak again. "You were so brave, standing up to Jane."

"Not really," said Amber. "Who's Mrs. MacRae's boss?"

"Her boss? Why—no one. She's the director."

"Well, but—somebody pays her. There's a committee, or something, right?"

"Oh, the trustees. They come out every few months and eat dinner and pat a few little ones on the head."

"Anybody ever run away?"

"Run away?" Ethel sounded suddenly alert. "But what would you do if you ran away?"

"Same thing I did before I got here," said Amber, with more confidence than she felt. "The question is, can it be done?"

"I—I suppose so." Ethel sounded doubtful. "There was a girl a few years ago, she just walked out one day—but I heard she lost her virtue and lived a dreadful life."

"Who'd you hear that from?"

"Miss Devine."

Amber snorted. "Would you trust her to tell the difference between a fun life and a dreadful one?"

Ethel was silent a long time. "N-no."

Amber yawned, trying to remember what else she had been going to ask; but Ethel spoke first again. "If you ran away, would you want to go by yourself?"

"I don't know," said Amber, surprised.

"Because—I've been thinking. I'm almost old enough to be sent out. And Grof is still so little—"

"*Hsst!*" came from the bed nearest the door. The room fell still. Amber heard footsteps in the hall, saw the doorknob turn and the door open to show a fat shape loom against the darkness. Mrs. Prine, come to check on them before she went to bed herself; or maybe she had heard something? Amber held her breath as she came in and walked up and down the room making sure all the windows were closed against the rain.

When she left, the tension went out of the room. Ethel rolled over and drew a deep, ragged breath. Amber thought she must be crying, but she didn't know what to do about it and lay still, embarrassed, until she fell asleep.

School at the orphanage was weird. About thirty kids sat in the room where she'd sewed sheets on Saturday, little ones in front, big ones in back. Amber wound up doing seventh-grade reading, fifth-grade spelling, seventh-grade math, and (what really ticked her off) third-grade history, because she couldn't name the presidents.

Most of the time was spent working assignments on small blackboards while Miss Devine had one class or another at the front of the room. Amber soon noticed that everyone stood their textbooks up on their desks so that Miss Devine couldn't see behind them. Doing the same, she tore a blank page out of her copybook and showed

Ethel how to make a paper airplane. Jane Henderson watched over her spelling book, and copied her. Her brother, Bob, copied Jane. Somebody else copied Ethel.

Soon paper airplanes zoomed across the schoolroom every time Miss Devine's back was turned. The class nearly burst with giggles and suspense. Would this one land safely on the target's desk? Would it overshoot and land in Miss Devine's lap, or catch in her hair, or (as Amber's demonstration model of a round airplane did) bounce off her nose as she turned? Would it sail, irrecoverable, out the window; or bounce back in the draft?

Miss Devine's face pinched thinner and meaner. By the end of the day, she'd slapped everybody in the place with a ruler—including Amber, three times, because she couldn't spell *mellifluous*. The sting remained in Amber's palm till after supper, but the only effect was to make her stubborn. Miss Devine deserved to be pestered to death with paper airplanes!

After school the girls did housework and the boys trooped out to the fields. More pointless dusting, sweeping, and polishing; Amber was glad to be sent to help Aunt Sally Manger in the kitchen, even though that soon proved to have its own drawbacks. She sat on the back steps, peeling potatoes, with Jane Henderson. Hot air from the kitchen beat against her back and sweat trickled down her front. Flies buzzed in and out as they pleased.

The kitchen smelled raw and foul with the smoke from the stove and the sweat of the people working. Aunt Sally Manger, her sleeves rolled up and her bandana dark with sweat, wielded a cleaver on a scarred wooden table, hacking a ham into frying slices. Amber staggered in with as many potatoes as she could carry. "Where do these go, ma'am?"

"That pot on the stove." Aunt Sally Manger waved her cleaver, and then brought it down, *bang!* through the ham, bone and all. "Don't put no salt in. I already did that."

Amber dumped the potatoes (already turning brown around the edges) into the iron pot, where a previous batch already bobbed among the first bubbles of boiling. Drops of water splashed out, spattering Amber's hands painfully. She yelped.

"Well, honey, don't drop 'em all in at once!" Aunt Sally Manger did not look up. "Anybody'd think you never fixed spuds before. Go grease those bread pans, now. Ethel's got the lard."

Ethel was mixing coarse yellow batter in a bowl as big around as a bike tire. The lard was white, smelly grease in a bucket, which Amber spread around in the pans with a stiff brush. "Don't we ever get any vegetables?" she asked, wrinkling her nose.

"What you think a spud is?" asked Aunt Sally Manger. "And corn bread—that's made out of vegetables."

"I mean—you know—carrots. Broccoli. Lettuce."

"Won't see none of that here," said Aunt Sally Manger, reaching over Amber's shoulder with a spatula and scooping out a hunk of lard. "Cost too much to buy, and too much trouble to grow, for all the people that'd need to eat them."

"But—we'll get sick if we don't eat vegetables."

"Don't tell me. Tell Miz MacRae. I cook what they give me."

"You don't even know how to peel a spud," sneered

Jane, dropping the last potatoes gently, one by one, into the pot, "or sew, or spell *mellifluous*. What do you know about illness?"

"I don't see what spelling *mellifluous* has to do with anything," retorted Amber, spreading lard with vigor.

"You act so high and mighty, like you know everything." Jane reached for the salt shaker.

"No need to fuss at each other," said Aunt Sally Manger, stirring the lard on the griddle over the stove so it would melt faster. "I don't want to hear any fighting in my kitchen. And don't you put any more salt in that water! I had it just right."

Jane Henderson turned with a flounce of her pinafore. "I don't have to care what you want, you old black thing! I could complain to the committee about how uppity you are to us, and then they'd remove you."

Amber stopped greasing the bread pan, expecting Aunt Sally Manger to explode; but all she did was frown at the griddle like a thundercloud. Jane's smug look was more than Amber could stand. "Not if Ethel, Aunt Sally, and I said you were lying," she said. "That'd be three against one."

"Let's all hush and forget about it." The cook slapped a slice of ham onto the griddle. "Seems to me a white orphan and a colored cook'll be about the same to the committee; close enough to where we maybe don't want to find out who they'll believe. You got those pans greased yet, Amber?"

Dinner did not taste any better for Amber having helped prepare it, though at least the potatoes had the right amount of salt for a change. Afterward she trooped out with the others, and finally found out what went on during an exercise period.

It was like recess without a playground. The smaller children played ring games, the big girls walked around and around the house in pairs, and the big boys showed off, with hand slapping, tug-of-war, and even rooster fighting. When Bob Henderson, a smaller boy mounted on his shoulders, chased another team all the way around the building, Amber kept expecting someone to come out and put a stop to it; but nothing happened.

Grof ran straight up to Ethel as soon as he saw her, grinning and grunting. He hung on to Ethel's hand as they walked around the building, watching everything with round eyes.

"How long have y'all been stuck here?" Amber asked.

"Oh, ages. Since I was eight and he was two. There was scarlet fever, and it took everybody, except us."

"What, even your aunts and uncles?"

"I still have an aunt and uncle in Boerne, but they have seven children already." Ethel's face looked as old as a grandmother's. "I don't think Grof remembers the family. I tell him about them, but you can't tell how much he understands. If he understands anything."

Amber watched Grof, trotting between them, holding hands with each, and wished Mom were here. Amber felt like she ought to be able to help, but she didn't want to make anything worse, meddling ignorantly.

"Did it take him a long time to learn to walk?" she asked.

Ethel shook her head. "No. He walked beautifully, and learned to use his spoon. He'd started to talk clearly when the fever came; and since then he stopped. That's why I think it must be the orphanage. Until then he was as normal as anybody."

Grof let go of Amber's hand and pointed upward, grinning. The girls looked up, to see a huge bird drifting overhead—a chicken hawk or maybe a vulture; Amber couldn't tell. "Bird," she said. "That's a bird, Grof."

Ethel petted his head. "Thank you for showing us, Grof. Can you say bird? That's a bird."

They had made another couple of circuits of the house, talking about the advantages of running away from the orphanage at night as opposed to during the day, when the shouting started. Grof's shoe had come unbuttoned, and Ethel was directing Amber's attention to the competent way he bent down to button it himself, when the noise made the two girls jump. A ring had formed between the two outhouses (or privies, as Ethel called them), and people were shouting and jumping up and down. "I wonder who's fighting," said Amber.

"Only one way to find out!" Ethel stepped toward the ruckus, then stepped back to tug Grof to his feet.

When they arrived Bob Henderson was trying to make another boy, Jake, eat dirt. It was the most interesting sight since Amber had come to the orphanage; and until Mr. Huff, the man who supervised the boys in the fields, hauled away both boys, she had no time to think of anything else.

Even then she might not have realized what she had noticed, except that she and Ethel had lost hold of Grof's hands, and he was standing, bewildered, with his back to them. "Grof!" called Ethel. "Over here!"

He did not respond. She went over to him and laid her hand on his shoulder, at which he jumped, looked up, and relaxed.

"Oh!" cried Amber. "Helen Keller had scarlet fever!"

"What'd you say?" asked Ethel.

"Nothing," said Amber, unable to remember whether Ethel could have heard of Helen Keller. "Hang on. I want to try something." She clapped her hands as hard as she could next to Grof's ear. He did not react. She snapped her fingers. Nothing; only he turned his head and reached for her fingers. "Yell at him," Amber instructed Ethel, "now, while he's looking at me." She started moving her fingers in the deaf alphabet.

Ethel, used to being bossed, took a deep breath and yelled: "Grof!" Her little brother continued to watch Amber's fingers.

"That's it! We've got to go show Mrs. MacRae!"

"Show her what?" asked Ethel, following as Amber set off for the house, Grof in tow. Amber's boots clattered on the wooden steps, and Ethel's voice rose to a squeak. "But—we can't go in now! The rules—"

"This is lots more important than the rules!" Afire with her discovery, she led them noisily to the office and banged on the door. It opened abruptly, and Mrs. Prine glared down at her. Behind her were Mrs. MacRae, at her desk, and Miss Devine, stiff as a stick in a straight-back chair. "What are you doing inside?" she demanded. "We are conducting a meeting."

"We found out what's wrong with Grof!" Amber pulled him forward; he had fallen back with a squeak at sight of Mrs. Prine. "You have trouble with him because he doesn't do as he's told, right? And he hasn't learned to talk yet, right? And his folks all died of—"

"Amber Burak!" interrupted Mrs. MacRae, "you will cease this disruptive behavior at once!"

Amber got a grip. "Sorry," she gasped, bobbing. "I

99

mean, sorry, ma'am. But as soon as I figured out what was wrong, I—"

"This is the boy I was discussing with you," said Mrs. Prine. "He shouldn't be with normal children."

A ledger lay open on the desk. Mrs. MacRae glanced into it. "And the girl in the hall—you're his sister, Ethel?"

Ethel bobbed nervously. "Yes, ma'am." Her eyes wanted to watch the floor, but with effort she raised them and looked Mrs. MacRae in the face. "Amber was so excited, and she was pulling Grof. . . . I told her it was against the rules, ma'am, but she said this was more important."

Miss Devine sniffed.

"It is," Amber said. "Lookit. Grof's got his eyes on Mrs. Prine, right?" He was watching the matron with a look of terror; but it didn't seem to bother her, the fat old hag. "Watch what happens when I clap my hands next to his ear." She suited the deed to the word.

"I don't see anything," said Mrs. Prine.

"No, that's the point!" She whirled and clapped her hands next to Ethel's ear. The girl started. "See! If you hear a loud noise, you jump! You can't help it! Grof doesn't talk because he can't! The scarlet fever made him deaf!"

She faced them triumphantly; but Mrs. Prine snorted. "You've been here all of three days, missy, and you know what's wrong with him better than I do? He's been in my nursery for four years; and I say he's a simpleton."

"This chit is a ringleader," said Miss Devine, her mouth so steel-trappish Amber expected to hear her teeth snap. She produced a battered paper Concorde jet. "I never saw one of these contraptions before, but no sooner does she show up than they overrun the schoolroom. She neither sews nor spells, her Bible training is deficient, and she is impertinent. This is merely another piece of mischief."

"But why would I—" began Amber.

Mrs. Prine interrupted her with a slap. "Children should be seen, not heard."

"Then why does it bug you that Grof can't talk?" asked Amber, and wished she hadn't.

Mrs. Prine slapped her again. Each cheek now had a matching burn. Grof began to cry. "Ethel, take him outside," Mrs. Prine said.

Ethel hustled Grof away. Amber gritted her teeth. Mrs. MacRae was watching her, sadly. "I am ready to listen to you, Amber. Have you any explanation for your conduct?"

"I already told you," said Amber. "Ma'am. He can't hear. I figured it was more important for you to know that than for me to follow a little rule. Ma'am."

"Rules exist for reasons," said Mrs. MacRae. "It is against the rules for children to return to the house during the exercise period, or to disturb me in my office. Do you understand that?"

"Yes, ma'am." Amber sighed. "If you want to switch me, fine. But the important thing—"

"The important thing is that you learn to do as you are told and speak respectfully to your elders. The committee will be visiting soon, including Mrs. Bauer, who sent you here. I would hate to have to give her a bad report of your conduct. Mrs. Prine, will you put Amber in the dining hall, where she can reflect on her behavior between now and evening prayers?"

As Mrs. Prine led her away, she saw Mrs. MacRae turn

to Miss Devine and pick up the paper airplane. "You say these objects flew?" she asked. The door closed. Mrs. Prine twisted Amber's arm behind her back and marched her to the dining hall. Bob and Jake were already there, sitting unnaturally straight and still. "It'll be a painful evening for everyone." Mrs. Prine smiled nastily, and left them.

"So what'd you do?" demanded Bob.

"Tried to do them a good turn," said Amber. "What's that in your pocket?"

"Nothing."

"Fine," said Amber, fed up. "Do they switch us at prayers?"

"Right." He grinned meanly. "On our legs. The stockings don't help."

"I bet God gets a real kick out of it." She went to the kitchen, where Aunt Sally Manger was washing the dishes, and her husband, Otis, smoked a corncob pipe. Amber had never seen a real corncob pipe before, but she was too mad to pay attention to it. "Ma'am," she said, "what's the committee?"

"Good night, what are you doing in here? You're supposed to be getting your exercise."

"I know. What's the committee Jane was talking about while we were making dinner?"

Otis blew a smoke ring. "Bunch of rich white folks," he said. "They won't do you no good."

"Could Jane really complain to them?"

The cook rinsed the griddle. "She could try. They come round every so often, pat y'all on the head, hear you say your verses. But you know they'll listen to Mrs. MacRae, not you."

"But if we all complained, they'd have to listen."

Aunt Sally Manger shrugged. "You get on back in the dining hall before Mrs. Prine catches you and we all get in trouble!"

Amber did as she was told. She was in a slow burn as the children filed in, as Mrs. MacRae made a speech about how badly the three children had behaved, as Bob let loose the mouse in his pocket and it ran across the open Bible, to the suppressed delight of every child. The switching hurt more than she would have thought possible, but she gritted her teeth and took it quietly. She didn't hear the prayers or the Bible reading because she was thinking too hard.

Sore and mad, she limped to the dorm with the other girls, who looked at her out of the sides of their eyes. As they undressed, Luella said: "Ethel says you reckon Grof is deaf."

"He is." Amber struggled with her shoe buttons.

"I think you're right," said Luella. "Grof isn't stupid. He makes handkerchief dolls beautifully, and he helps the smallest ones learn to walk. His being deaf explains everything much better."

Ethel brightened.

"So what if he is?" Jane sneered. "There's no home for the deaf here. It's cheaper to put him with the simpletons than buy him a train ticket, and that way Mrs. Prine won't have to admit that she was wrong. Mrs. MacRae won't do anything."

"I know it," said Amber, three buttons popping off her boot. "That's why we're going to!"

CHAPTER NINE

Proper Placement

Ada kept the hair ribbon in her bureau drawer, taking it out and staring at it from time to time when she was supposed to be doing her homework. The creature in the well must have thrown it to her for a reason; but until she puzzled out that reason, she could not give it to the Buraks. They would certainly not rest until the well was drained or dug up—and then what would become of her chance to return home? She hated to grieve the Buraks; but she had parents of her own to consider, and, as Violet pointed out with heartless practicality, if Amber's body were in the well, it could be retrieved as easily after Ada returned as before.

May in 1991 was a warm and humid month, without, it seemed to Ada, nearly enough flowers. Mimosa bloomed in the front yard of the shelter, and roses next door; but no poppies, no yards full of bluebonnets, not even any dandelions to speak of. This, with the absence of china trees and the presence of unreasonably tall pecans and live oaks on every hand, kept her from feeling that she was in her hometown.

She discovered why the poppies had vanished one day when the police came to school and gave a lesson in recognizing dangerous drugs. Ada was appalled. Laudanum—which she herself had administered to Odett when she was cranky with fever—was now declared as dangerous as poison, and the gorgeous orange poppies from which opium could be obtained had been deliberately discouraged within the city! Ada listened with mounting horror to the list of perilous substances that apparently prowled the streets waiting to enslave innocent children. Coke, crack, ice, LSD, PCP—she grew quite ill contemplating it all.

"Why do you put up with it?" she demanded of Violet as they left the auditorium, as if her friend were responsible for all the aspects of her era.

Violet shrugged. "What do you expect me to do? Anyway, the cops make it sound worse than it is. All you got to do is keep your head and not let anybody push you into taking the stuff."

"They kept talking about pushers," said Ada, hugging her books as if they could shield her from the slings and arrows of this strange century. "Is that what you said Cody's uncle was? A—pusher—who sells this devil's stuff?"

"That's right," said Violet. "Look, don't worry about it. He won't knock you down and stick a needle in your arm."

That was not what was troubling Ada. She knew her father kept not only laudanum, but opium, morphine, and hashish in his drugstore. If Violet knew that, would she say Pappa was a pusher? Pappa was nothing like the criminals described in the police lecture—but Ada could not risk losing Violet's friendship.

Violet and Ada went to the school library every chance they got, and read every book in it that touched on the subject of travel between times and worlds—what Violet called dimensions. Ada shivered with anticipatory wonder every time she opened one of these books.

In books children who traveled in time either had no control over the process or had a set of rules. So long as they behaved in the proper manner, they would be able to go and return as they pleased. Neither of these cases applied to Ada. The books about travel to other worlds were more encouraging. Dorothy and her friends reached Oz via any number of natural disasters, and returned to America in equally varied ways. The children who traveled back and forth to Narnia likewise found many routes—one of them, a well! Normally, the characters had some task to accomplish, assigned by Providence, after which they were allowed (or were forced) to go home.

"Suppose I were brought here to find Amber?" she suggested to Violet one evening, having completely failed to grasp the meaning of her assigned reading in her science text, and having fallen back upon the bed to rest her eyes.

"Suppose you were?" asked Violet, tilting her chair and stretching backward till her braids hung down straight. "Who'd send you? And what'd they expect you to do? The police and the child welfare services and half the grown-ups in the world are tramping after her. And how does Amber rate getting special help called in, when Heidi didn't? She died, and no fairies tried to help her out!"

That had troubled Ada, too. "Can you think of another reason why the fairy would give me her hair ribbon?"

"To let you know Amber's body is blocking your way home?"

106

Ada shuddered. "I don't believe that. It's too horrible."

"Nothing's too horrible to happen."

"I don't believe it, all the same."

"Neither do I," admitted Violet, sitting up straight again. "So let's think about this idea. If you got called across a hundred years to find Amber, there'd have to be a good reason." Violet scratched. "Dadgum skeeters. They're all over!"

"There's not near as many as I'm used to," said Ada. The telephone in the lower hall rang, distant and shrill. "And you seem to have killed off all the flies."

Violet snorted. "My dad says—"

A knock came on the door, immediately followed by Loyce sticking her head in. "Phone for you, Ada."

"For me?" Ada sat up.

"That's what I said, isn't it? It's Ms. Burak."

Wondering nervously what Mrs. Burak could want to speak to her about, Ada followed Loyce downstairs to the telephone. This instrument was entirely unlike the one in Pappa's store, but she had seen people use ones like it on TV, so she got the earpiece and mouthpiece in their proper places. She had to cover one ear with her hand to shut out the TV, which was a constant background noise in this part of the house. "Hello? This is Ada Bauer."

"Hi, Ada." The voice was clear and recognizable. "I'm sorry I haven't been able to see you, but I want to let you know what's going on. Have you ever met a Dr. Cunningham?"

"Yes, ma'am, once," said Ada. "A woman doctor with yellow hair."

Mrs. Burak asked when this had been, and what they had spoken about. "This is worse than I thought," she said eventually. "If she'd never seen you at all I could use that as a lever, but now—look, here's the deal. You can't stay in the shelter much longer, and since we can't find your parents, we'll need a court order to place you."

Ada felt queasy. "They won't—you won't let them send me to an asylum, will you?"

"I wish I could tell you they'll put you away over my dead body, but it's not up to me. Dr. Cunningham is the staff psychiatrist, and she recommends that you undergo treatment—which means the state mental facilities."

Ada sank onto the chair beside the phone. "But—I'm not mad. Why does Dr. Cunningham say I am?"

"As far as I can tell, she's basing her judgment solely on your story about being from a hundred years ago. Everything else supports my recommendation that you be placed in a foster home, but you did insist on repeating that story several times, for the record, and the judge can't ignore it."

"I'll—I'll take it back," said Ada.

"I thought you might. I'm trying to set up an appointment for you to see Dr. Cunningham again. Her caseload is way too heavy, which is why she didn't interview you properly in the first place. I can't blame her for that." Her voice gave her words the lie; Ada could tell that Mrs. Burak blamed Dr. Cunningham a great deal. "I'll do whatever it takes to get you an interview, but then it's up to you. You have to tell the truth, Ada. At least enough to prove you're okay."

"Yes, ma'am," said Ada, softly. Mrs. Burak talked some more, but she scarcely listened. Ada would rather die than tell a lie—but that didn't seem to be one of her options.

Violet was leaning over the banister when Ada replaced the receiver on the telephone. In the living room, the TV laughed. "Dr. Cunningham wants to put me in a madhouse," Ada said.

"Bummer, bummer, bummer," said Violet. "Like we don't have enough problems. I wanted to get a little TV in tonight."

Ada rose, despite the limp-noodle sensation in her limbs, and climbed the stairs to their room. "I'm sorry," she said. "Mrs. Burak's arranging for me to see Dr. Cunningham and convince her I'm not mad. Go watch TV. I can work out a lie on my own." Someone behind one of the closed doors was playing a music machine—a radio—a tiny bit too loud; the underlying rhythm thumped in the walls and floor. Ada hurled herself across the bed and stared at the floor. "Lying's a mortal sin."

Violet closed the door and flopped down beside her. "If the grown-ups'd give you a chance, you could prove it to them same as you did to me. My dad says when the Man pushes you into a corner where you got to do something wrong to get out, you should pick the thing that helps you the most and not worry about it."

"I can't help it," said Ada, "but Mamma and Pappa will be so worried—it would be a worse sin to leave them like that."

"Atta girl!" Violet slapped her on the back, and pulled Ada's ring binder off the nightstand. "I don't really mind missing TV, you know." She fished in the pencil bag. "We need a real bugger of a lie, and that takes practice. So listen up. I may not be around next time you need one."

Ada, appalled by this thought, sat up and paid attention. Violet had apparently thought about lying a lot; she had lots of principles worked out, like "Keep it simple" and "Remember who you're lying to." Before the evening was over she had added: "Remember who's doing the lying," because Ada's conscience and the state of her knowledge were terrible stumbling blocks. The importance of Violet's third principle of lying, "Use as much truth as you can," soon became evident. There was no disguising the fact that Ada had not had a twentieth-century education, and she could not state even the simplest lie without something in her face, voice, or posture giving her away.

By bedtime they had an unsatisfactory first draft of a lie, and Ada had committed the principles to memory so that Violet could destroy the paper on which they were written. Teeth and hair brushed, alarm clock set, lights out, and all quiet—save for the monotonous crying of one of the children down the hall—Ada lay on her back staring into the dark, her brain whirling. Her stomach ached with fear and guilt. Guilt toward Mrs. Burak, and her family, and Dr. Cunningham, and God, and even—she realized, hearing a tired sigh—toward Violet.

"You're mighty kind to help me so much," she said.

"I heard that!" Violet agreed, flopping over loudly. "Mom says I like to show off, so I guess you're doing me a favor by being here to help."

This was not at all the response she had expected. "Still, you've been a generous friend to me."

"Knock it off," growled Violet. "Mom says if folks like us don't take care of each other, nobody else will."

"Folks like us?" The phrase struck her ear like a physical shock. She and Violet were nothing alike!

"Yeah. You know. The ones on the edges. The ones the rules don't work for." She sounded grown-up and angry. "We're all in crud together, and the people that're supposed to help us just trample us down more. So we got to help ourselves."

Ada, feeling cold, pulled up the covers. She wished the windows were open and that someone would turn off the air conditioning. "Mrs. Burak isn't trampling us."

"Naw. Dr. Cunningham is, though. And all the politicians, and things." Violet's voice trailed off.

Ada realized that Violet's tones, allowing for the modern accent, precisely echoed her own when repeating Mamma's arguments on women's rights, temperance, and such matters. "Do your parents agree on that?" she asked.

"Oh, sure." Violet yawned. "They agree on everything."

"That must be—pleasant." Ada awaited a response, got none, and asked: "Why aren't you with them?"

"The Man won't let me."

She sounded so bitter, Ada was afraid to ask; but Violet had never been in such a forthcoming mood before. "What man?"

"The Man. You know. The Man that runs things."

"You mean President Har—Bush?" Ada scraped together everything she could remember about the current president. The same day she had found Amber's hair ribbon, something had gone wrong with his heart, and the news story about it had eaten up almost all of the evening's TV. The grown-ups all seemed to like him because of a recent successful war, which was (in some obscure way) involved with yellow ribbons.

"No. The Man isn't one person. He's all of . . . my dad says, all of the white people; but it's not just that. The people that . . . that won't help us or let us help ourselves, you know?" Violet's voice groped. "Trust me, okay? We've got to help each other 'cause nobody else will."

Ada did not see what this had to do with Violet's not living at home. She lay still, turning it all over in her head, until she was almost asleep. Then an idea jolted her awake. "Violet!" she whispered.

"What?" Violet mumbled into her pillow.

"What if I promise you not to tell anyone the details of my history? I can say I can't tell Dr. Cunningham certain things because I gave my word not to. We pick out all the things I can say safely, and everything else is under the promise!"

Violet was quiet for a long time. "You're brilliant," she said. "She'll hate it."

"I don't care," said Ada, recklessly.

To Ada's disappointment, that was the last she heard of the matter for two weeks. At first she woke tense each morning, wondering if this were the day that would decide her fate; but soon the excitements of everyday life intervened. She did not work hard at school, since it seemed largely pointless. She had no groundwork for much that was covered in science and history, the English course was absurdly easy, and in math class she sat so far in back that she could barely read the board. In the required Spanish course she had started so hopelessly far behind that there was no question of her ever catching up.

Ada rather wanted to do well in typing, since the textbook writer claimed that the machine had been of the utmost importance in giving women employment. However she felt obscurely guilty at the notion of striving to excel—as if by securing a place in her new life, she would render less probable her return to her old.

So Ada devoted herself to reading useful books, and to her art class, conscious that she might never get a chance at such an accomplishment again. She even, after a fashion, made friends with a boy in art, who was shunned by others as a "nerd," but who had mastered the art of making drawings move.

All these matters having absorbed her attention, Ada suffered a small shock when, on the day her last science report was due, Loyce stopped her on the way to the bus with the sharp words: "Hang on! You've got to see Dr. Cunningham today."

"Do I?" Ada and Violet both pulled up short.

"I told you last night at dinner," said Loyce crossly.

"You did not," retorted Violet.

"Well, I'm telling you now. Jennifer's driving you, and I can't spare her, so get a move on." Loyce bustled off.

Ada felt as if her stomach had fallen out.

"It's about time," said Violet. "All you got to do is remember what we worked out. You'll be fine."

"Tip-top," nodded Ada, without conviction. "Will you—turn in my science report? And the math homework? And—"

"Sure, sure." Violet took her binder and report covers from her, leaving her with three textbooks and a book from the library. "Go on. And promise me—"

Ada gulped. "I promise, I will tell no one any detail

about my history that you have not previously approved. Honor bright."

"Good. And don't talk like that. It makes you sound prissy." Violet hopped into the bus.

"Ada! Jennifer's waiting!" Loyce yelled from the porch.

Downtown, familiar limestone buildings were too close to towering newcomers of glass or brick. The green river was too far below the level of the streets, and the streets had too much pavement. Where were the hay wagons, the candy and tamale sellers, the buggies and drays and horses and dirt and flies? Ada was dangerously near being homesick for flies by the time Jennifer paid to leave the car in a field of asphalt.

Dr. Cunningham's office was in the top of a limestone building. Ada thought it might date from her day, but the offices within were pure twentieth-century. Jennifer settled her in a plastic chair, spoke to a woman at a desk, and returned smiling. Jennifer smiled habitually, so Ada did not place much reliance on it.

"I've got to get back to the shelter now," said Jennifer. "Dr. Cunningham had to squeeze you in, but she'll see you just as soon as she can, and somebody'll take you on to school. Okay?"

Ada nodded. What else could she do?

She waited while people who had come later than she had went in ahead of her, while parents and children argued, while she finished her library book, while the TV mounted high on the wall nattered, getting duller with each show. She got hungry. Anxiety heated and hardened inside her until it resembled anger.

When Dr. Cunningham emerged from her office, Ada rose automatically, but the doctor took no notice, stopping instead at the desk. "I'm running down for a bite," she said, in a low voice. "Give me half an hour." She strode for the door.

It was not a good time, but Ada did not know when the next time might be. "Dr. Cunningham—"

"I'm going to lunch."

"May I go with you, ma'am? I have my lunch money."

Dr. Cunningham looked at her. "Who are you?"

"Ada Bauer, ma'am. I've been here since eight-thirty."

"Bauer?" She looked blank, then angry. "Oh, you." Suddenly she laughed, mirthlessly. "Sure. Why should I get a half hour to myself? Come on."

The interview, conducted over sandwiches and milk bought from machines, was less frightful than Ada had anticipated. The sandwiches were even worse than most of the food Ada had eaten during the twentieth century, but Dr. Cunningham listened to all Ada had to say. Her parents were dead a long time ago. She had never been enrolled in the current version of the Texas public school system. She had run away from her legal guardians (what else could it be called?), but held herself unable to give details of her reasons or their identity due to a solemn promise made to a dear friend.

Dr. Cunningham did not see the necessity of keeping this promise as clearly as Ada had hoped, but was more interested in Ada's reasons for telling her original story. "Why'd you pick something so weird? You couldn't expect anyone to believe it."

"I didn't know what to say," said Ada. "I'd been reading a book, about traveling in time, and I thought—well, it didn't work the way I planned."

Dr. Cunningham nodded, as if she understood. "You

wanted attention, and when you didn't get any it wasn't fun anymore." She finished her sandwich and brushed the crumbs onto the floor. "Remember this, next time you make up a story. Now I can't get out of testing you. After all, you could still be lying because Grace filled you up with horror stories about the mental homes. You want a candy bar? My treat."

Ada accepted, feeling better as soon as she bit into the chocolate. She hadn't tasted anything this good since losing her *peloncillo*! Fortified, she took written tests asking embarrassing questions, then waited again, till Dr. Cunningham's assistant could watch her match pegs in holes and identify shapes in ink blots.

"I'll give you a lift," said Dr. Cunningham, shoving a wad of papers into a desk as Ada stopped by her door to tell her she was finally (it was after six) finished. "I'll take your tests home, work them up in my so-called free time."

"That's very good of you," said Ada politely.

"Tell Ms. Burak that."

Dr. Cunningham's car was cramped, the backseat piled with papers, files, and magazines. "Ms. Burak come see you often?" she asked as they entered traffic.

"No, ma'am. She spoke to me on the phone once, and I was in her group when we searched for Amber."

Dr. Cunningham glanced sideways at her. "They've about given up on Amber, you know. They think she's probably dead."

Ada had never done anything about her idea that she might have been sent here to find Amber. "That's terrible," she said.

"You look like Amber. Did you know that?"

116

"We have the same color eyes and hair, that's all."

"Mmm." The sky was trying to rain, but only managed a few heavy drops. "There's no telling what'll happen after I evaluate your test results, Ada. I don't want you to get your hopes up and then blame me when it doesn't work out."

"No, ma'am," said Ada, for lack of anything better to say.

"The thing is, if you don't go to State, I don't know where they can put you. Grace as good as told me she didn't have a foster home lined up." She slipped her eyes sideways at Ada again. "Best thing would be to tell us who your guardians are."

"A promise is a promise," said Ada, primly.

CHAPTER TEN

The Committee

Jane summed up the universal opinion when she said, in response to Amber's second day of attempting to drum up support for Grof, "We'd get switched from here to breakfast if Mrs. Prine caught us crying her down." No one could get past that.

"Mrs. Prine's decided he's feebleminded, and she don't let us call her wrong," Luella said, glumly, during exercise period.

"We don't have to call her wrong, the committee does," said Amber. "If we can prove to them—"

"But we can't prove it." Luella shuffled her feet as they walked under the barred nursery windows. "And even if we could, she'd say he's feebleminded as well as deaf, on account of his not learning things."

"If I looked after the little ones, I'd teach him right quick," said Ethel, impatiently.

"Teach him what?"

"Deaf alphabet," said Amber. "Watch." She stood between Grof and the windows. Ethel squatted to his level, and spelled his name with her fingers, saying the letters out loud. Grof grinned and copied her. Amber was almost sure she'd remembered all the letters right, and Ethel had picked them up quickly.

"What's the point of that?" asked Luella.

"It's a way for deaf people to talk," said Amber.

"But he's only mimicking."

"That's what we need you for," said Ethel, tapping Grof on the chest and repeating the handsigns. "If you learn to sign, you can talk to him in the nursery and he'll learn faster."

"I can't learn those." Luella watched Grof's fingers move.

"It's not hard. Ethel's learned the whole alphabet since the day before yesterday." Amber tried to think of something that would make Luella want to learn. "It's good for talking in class. You hold your fingers below the desk"— she demonstrated against her thigh—"and spell what you want to say."

Luella looked interested. Grof tugged Ethel's skirt, pointed to himself, and spelled his name. "Right!" cried Ethel, hugging him.

"Now I think about it, he already knows some signs," said Luella as Ethel and Grof continued to perform and praise. "When it's nap time, we tell the little ones to be quiet, and I put my finger on my lip like that"—she made the gesture—"and he lies down. And if you shout at him not to do something, he keeps right on, but if you shake your head, he stops."

"See? You've already started the job."

"But if Mrs. Prine catches on . . ."

Amber sighed, and reached into her pocket. "Do you like candy, Luella?"

The other girl's face changed. "I guess I like it some."

Amber pulled out an atomic fireball. "You like cinnamon?"

Luella licked her lips. "I guess I would."

"I've got two pieces of the most excellent cinnamon candy in the world." She really had three left, but one must be saved to try again at the well. If she ever got back to the well. "You can have one now, and the other after Grof learns three words."

Luella held out her hand.

"It kind of bites at first," warned Amber; too late. Luella's eyebrows shot up at the shock of the initial flavor.

"Look, y'all!" called Ethel. She tapped her own chest, and Grof's fingers moved, carefully—E-T-H-E-L. "He knows my name now! Grof, you're a blue-eyed daisy!"

Miss Devine looked out of a lower window, too far away to see the details of her face, but Amber felt uncomfortable. "We better go back to walking," she said.

No one discussed it, but all the girls felt that it would be a bad thing for the grown-ups to catch them teaching Grof to sign. It turned out to be easy to disguise. Once Luella, Ethel, and Amber started signing behind Miss Devine's back, the practice spread as rapidly as the paper airplanes (or "airplies," as the girls called them) had.

Luella earned her fireball at the end of the first week, when Grof showed himself able to spell not only his name and his sister's, but *Luella*, *Amber*, *doll*, *hello*, and *Prine*—the last of which he always finished off by twisting up his face as if he were tasting something bad. It wasn't absolutely certain that he understood the connection between

120

his finger motions and reality, but he at least never spelled *Ethel* when pointing to Amber.

Luella sucked the fireball more easily this time. "You've done a real good job," Amber told her as they walked slowly around the house behind Ethel and Grof, who were signing at each other happily. "I wish I had more candy."

"It's all right." Luella spelled as she spoke. "I like getting more practice than the others, so I can sign faster."

"Good," said Amber. She wished they didn't have to walk so slowly. The evening was lightly humid and smelled like growing things, just right for playing Frisbee with Dad or batting tennis balls back and forth with Mom or . . .

Grof ran up to her flourishing an orange flower with one hand, spelling P-O-P-P-Y with the other.

He continued to improve daily; but this was the only thing Amber could find to be cheerful about. She got used to the smell of the orphanage and learned to braid her own hair so it wouldn't be so tight; she got to where she could use the chamber pot or the outhouse without wanting to throw up; and she learned to fasten her boots without popping off all the buttons (requiring her to laboriously sew them back on); but she wished she'd never had to learn any of these things. School was a pain in the neck, with Miss Devine hitting people for perfectly ordinary mistakes. Amber didn't think much of the sentences she assigned for spelling practice, either—"The laws of nature are sustained by the immediate presence and agency of God"! She was pretty sure assigning that sentence was unconstitutional.

Amber had never thought much about religion before, but now she was becoming hostile to the concept, at least of Christianity. Prayers every night, Bible verses to memorize, God and Jesus slipped into the schoolwork, and then church every Sunday! Mostly it was only boring, and some of the girls seemed to like it. Sometimes, though, the preacher said things that made Amber so mad she was shaking all over by the time church let out. He devoted one whole sermon to the reasons all Jewish people would go to hell, and he talked about women submitting to their husbands till she wanted to gag.

Amber could have lived with the food, though she soon vowed never to eat ham or corn bread again once she got home, and she could have withstood the onslaughts of bugs and the telltale traces of mice all over the orphanage, if only she had even for half an hour been by herself.

The orphanage held no place to hide. From the time she rolled out of bed in the morning to the time she fell asleep at night, Amber was always with someone. Even the outhouse had two seats. "Do you ever get tired of looking at people?" she asked Ethel at dinner one evening, surveying the mechanically moving forks all around.

"No," said Ethel, sounding surprised. "What people?"

"Any people. All people. Don't you ever wish they'd all go away and leave you alone for a while?"

"I wish they'd go away and leave me and Grof to ourselves, sometimes," said Ethel. "Except you, of course. And Luella. We'd have to have somebody else, because one person would need to look after Grof, and one person would need to make a living."

"No, I mean don't you ever want to just be by yourself? For a little while, not forever."

"What for?"

"Oh—read." Look at TV. "Laze around." Were jigsaws and crosswords invented yet? "Think. That sort of thing."

Ethel shook her head, chewing determinedly at the bite in her mouth. She was probably stuck with a piece of gristle.

"I'm so tired of seeing people's faces," continued Amber. "I'd almost like to get in trouble with Miss Devine and skip supper again, just to be by myself."

Ethel scratched her nose, passing a piece of gristle from her mouth to her palm and thence to her plate. "I'm sorry you're tired of us," she said, in a small voice.

"Not you," Amber said. "This whole place. I'd like to have a little peace to think in, that's all." She stared glumly at the corn bread crumbs on her plate.

"Think in church," suggested Ethel. "You don't like to listen to the preacher, anyway. Have you decided how to get Grof to the committee?"

Amber frowned. "How does the committee visit work, anyway? I can't make a plan if I don't know what to expect."

"Well—they come in the morning, and the littlest girls give them bouquets. Mrs. MacRae serves tea in the parlor. They have a girl to wait on them, and Mrs. Prine picks an extra girl to mind the nursery so she can go down. Then they tour the dorms, and the nursery, and go to the classrooms to hear us recite. They usually bring presents for the nursery. Then they have lunch—it's a tip-top day for lunch—and people make speeches and they all go home."

"Hmm." Amber drank her milk without tasting it. "Who waits on them in the parlor? Jane?"

"Usually. And Jane Williams helps Luella in the nursery."

"How does Miss Devine pick who recites?"

"Whoever's farthest up the class, one girl and one boy. It was Molly and Sam last time. Molly recited 'The Defense of the Alamo' and Sam said the Declaration of Independence."

Molly had been sent to the infirmary that morning, her face so red and sore Amber would not have been surprised to see it peel off. Amber and Ethel were both in the cluster of top readers remaining after cutting out her and Jane Henderson. "You have to be head of the class this next time," Amber said firmly.

"What use is it for me to recite?"

"See, what we do is, you memorize whatever Miss Devine puts in front of you, but when the committee comes, you do a speech about Grof, instead." Amber regarded her last, fatty piece of ham doubtfully. At home she would have left it on her plate; but here she was always hungry. She grimaced and speared it.

Ethel swallowed. "In—in front of Miss Devine?"

"If you start off with something really attention-grabbing, the committee won't let her stop you," said Amber. She hoped. She took the ham, chewed twice, and swallowed, feeling the fat creep nastily down her throat.

Mrs. MacRae wiped her mouth, preparing to stand and give the prayer. Those children who had not finished shoved their remaining food into their mouths and chewed frantically.

"I don't—I'm sorry, Amber," whispered Ethel. "I don't think I could. Not with Miss Devine watching."

"Oh, come on! He's your little brother."

"I know." Ethel looked miserable, and her words were almost drowned in the scraping of benches on the floor as everyone stood for grace. She signed quickly while they were bowing their heads and folding their hands: "Afraid."

Amber sighed. Why was everybody here such a chicken? She considered their alternatives as they filed into the yard and waited for Grof. "Okay," she said. "I'll do it, then."

"Miss Devine will never put you at the head of the class," Ethel pointed out. "She says you're a ringleader."

"She won't have a choice," said Amber. "Everybody else is going to be down with a cold."

They arranged it that very day, catching the other viable girl candidates in the yard and using whatever form of persuasion would do the trick. Ethel taught Grof to spell their names on the spot, which gained their sympathy; and Amber could think of all kinds of advantages to head colds and laryngitis. "You don't have to get sick unless she starts leaning on you to recite," she pointed out. "You can probably get out of memorizing anything for her, and—"

"And Aunt Sally Manger'll make you peppermint tea with honey," added Luella, her round face shining at the mere thought; though it sounded like a bogus combination to Amber.

"But if we all suddenly lose our voices when she wants us to recite, she'll suspect something," protested one girl.

"It doesn't have to be sudden." Amber had it worked out by now. "We'll all wake up with sore throats for a week or so, and then as soon as she favors one of us to recite, that person gets worse. Everybody else stays well—or, if you want, one of them can come down with it, too, and that'll look more natural."

By the end of the day, they had promises from everyone Miss Devine was likely to pick on. The girls had even promised not to tell Jane Henderson, though it was clear from the way she watched people's faces that she knew something was up. She read from *Lady Audley's Secret* and blew out her candle without approaching Amber, though.

"Amber," whispered Ethel.

"What?" Amber waved away a tickle that might be a mosquito on her nose.

"What if it doesn't work?"

Amber groaned. "Why are you such a worrywart, Ethel? It'll work. Why wouldn't it?"

"I don't know. But what if it doesn't?"

"Then we'll run away." Amber'd been planning to do that anyway, as soon as she figured out how. She'd rather be on her own, but if the committee didn't stop Mrs. Prine from sending Grof to the retarded school, she wouldn't be able to desert him and Ethel and not feel guilty.

"Really run away?" Ethel sounded as if she were talking about something strange and wonderful. "That'd be daisy. How would we do it?"

Amber flopped over and punched her pillow, wanting to scream. "This idea hasn't failed yet! Go to sleep, can't you?"

"Very well," said Ethel, happily.

Amber lay awake a long time, trying to think, but instead falling into a rut in which the same ideas and images repeated over and over, until she fell asleep and dreamed of the same things—home, the well, and the mysterious behavior of wishes.

Only two days later, after the girls had fulfilled their promises by complaining loudly to one another about morning sore throats, Mrs. MacRae announced an upcoming visit from the committee. "I know we all want to look our best," she said, smiling grimly, "so we will all work extra hard, to show our benefactors how well we are profiting from their kindness."

The expression that went around the table didn't look grateful. "Extra housework," Ethel spelled against her skirt for Amber's benefit.

Anything made of cloth—curtains, sheets, towels, napkins, whatever—was taken out to be aired and the cupboards dusted. Aunt Sally Manger supervised a complete overhaul of the kitchen, herself undertaking the finicky and endless task of polishing Mrs. MacRae's silver tea service. Floors were waxed. Hinges were oiled. The big girls and boys risked their necks washing windows with rags dipped in a nasty substance called coal oil.

To make room for all this housekeeping, Miss Devine shortened her classes, except for Sam, chosen to recite for the boys, and a succession of girls, all of whose voices died on command. One effect of this that Amber had not foreseen was that her allies got out of the worst of the housework, leaving more for the others to do. If word ever got out, Amber was not going to be popular; and she didn't like the way Jane looked at her when Mary Evans began to croak convincingly in the middle of the first verse of Tennyson's "Crossing the Bar."

Miss Devine held out one more whole day after that; but Mary Evans was only eleven, and nobody remained except younger children, Jane, and Amber. Friday morning, looking more like a steel trap than ever, Miss Devine looked over the row of girls in the back of the room, each with a piece of red flannel around her throat, and squared her shoulders as if about to face an army. "This epidemic of quinsy is most ill-timed," she said, "but what cannot be cured must be endured. Jane Henderson, I would like you to recite for the committee a week from today—"

Amber clenched her fists under her desk.

"—but Mrs. MacRae wants you to serve tea for the ladies that morning, and does not wish to burden you with more than your share of work."

"I don't mind," said Jane Henderson, looking so sweet and dutiful that Amber longed to break her face in.

"Mrs. MacRae insists that it would not be fair to you." Miss Devine looked as if she thought Mrs. MacRae was little better than a criminal, worrying about fairness at a time like this. "Therefore, Amber Burak must recite that day. Amber, can you learn to say 'Crossing the Bar' in a week's time?"

"Yes, ma'am," said Amber, casting her eyes down and trying to sound small and doubtful. She had been working at it ever since Miss Devine picked it, and could say it in her sleep. "I believe so, ma'am. Don't you think Jane could—?"

"No, she could not!" Miss Devine slapped her own hand with the ruler she used both for pointing at the blackboard and for hitting people. "You will practice until you are flawless, and may heaven forfend that you come down with the quinsy!"

Amber acted like a good little orphan all that week, abandoning sign language, paper airplanes, and all forms of fidgeting. "What are you up to?" hissed Jane, as they scrubbed the front porch together the day before the committee arrived.

"I don't know what you mean," said Amber.

"Hmph!" grunted Jane. "Whatever it is, you watch out. You're not cock of the walk here."

Amber got the bucket of rinse water. It was hard not to dump it on Jane, but she managed.

At last the great day came. Miss Devine rang the bell earlier than usual. The lucky girls chosen to make the bouquets sat on the front porch working with bundles of poppies, Indian blanket, honeysuckle, and wild petunia. Everyone else polished their boots with cream of tartar and made one last sweep of the house (girls) and grounds (boys), putting in order things that looked in order already to Amber. When the boy sent down to the road to watch came running to the porch shouting that the committee was in sight, everyone hurried to line up on the porch.

The committee was seven ladies in an open carriage driven by a black man and drawn by two brown horses with black manes. All the ladies wore broad-brimmed hats that seemed in danger of flying off in the breeze, and dresses that were straight in front and trailed out behind. Mrs. Bauer looked tired and sad.

The committee members each got a bouquet from the littlest children, ranging from four to six and all, girls and boys, dressed in skirts. Grof, Amber noticed angrily, stood right in front of Mrs. Prine with her fingers digging into his shoulder. Poor kid must be too scared to move! The committee were polite about the flowers, Mrs. MacRae

129

made a little speech about how happy everyone was to see them, the orphans all curtsied or bowed, and the committee went indoors.

School did not go well that morning. The boys, resentful that none of them had had any chance of getting out of class to help with the nursery or the parlor, were deliberately stupid. Miss Devine was even less tolerant of mistakes than usual. The sore-throat girls could not keep their voices consistent. Ethel wrung her hands and forgot how to multiply. Amber's stomach hurt. She reread the speech she had prepared in the margins of her history book. It sounded totally dumb.

Finally they heard the committee trooping upstairs. Suddenly Amber wanted to giggle. She bit her lip and struggled to control herself as she obeyed Miss Devine's summons for the top reading class to come up. Herself at one end of the line, Sam at the other, they were just finished lining up in front of the desk when the door opened and Mrs. MacRae poked her head in. "Excuse us, Miss Devine," she said, in a voice not one bit like her usual one. "Shall we disturb your class if we come in and observe for one little moment?"

"Not at all," said Miss Devine, also in some stranger's voice. "I was about to ask the top class to recite the pieces they learned this week. Come in, by all means."

The committee lined up inside the door, looking polite or bored or intense, depending on who they were. Did they really believe they were coming in on a normal school day? Miss Devine pointed to Sam first, and he began reciting the Preamble to the Constitution. Jane Henderson slipped in behind the committee and took her place in the back of the room.

Amber caught Mrs. Bauer's eye, and smiled at her. She smiled back and wiggled her gloved fingers in a miniwave. Thus encouraged, Amber soon had herself under control and began to fear that the committee would get bored and leave before her turn came. However, they seemed to understand what was required of them, and stood patiently while Sam finished, and Miss Devine nodded. "Very good," she said, in that unnatural voice. "Let's see—Amber, I want to hear you recite 'Crossing the Bar.' "

Amber took a deep breath, stepped forward, pointed her toes out, clasped her hands in front of her in approved recitation posture, and promptly forgot every word of her speech. "I think it's a lot more important to talk about what's going to happen to Grof Schneider," she gabbled.

Miss Devine raised her ruler. Mrs. MacRae gasped. Knowing that speed was of the essence, Amber turned to the startled committee and plunged ahead.

"See, Grof's six years old and can't talk yet, so they're going to send him to a retarded home, but his big sister, Ethel, and I found out he's deaf because he had scarlet fever when he was a baby and that happens sometimes, so we've been teaching him the deaf alphabet and he's learning real fast, but Mrs. Prine doesn't like to be caught in a mistake and won't pay attention to us so Mrs. MacRae has to take her word over ours, you can't blame her for that" (Amber could and did; this was what Dad called diplomacy) "but I'm sure if you check it out you'll agree with Ethel and me" (Should that be Ethel and I? Too late!) "that he's plenty smart and needs a deaf school." She took a deep breath. "And Miss Devine can switch me all she wants. It was my . . . my" (Say it! she ordered herself sternly) "my Christian duty to let you know about him."

131

She got over that last hurdle, which she had planned on all along, only by thinking "Jewish" as hard as she could while her mouth said "Christian."

"And if she's switched, I . . . I should be switched, too," quavered Ethel, stepping out of her place in line. "He's my brother and I should have done this, but I was too afraid."

The look on Miss Devine's face was worth any number of switchings. "What is the meaning of this?" demanded Mrs. MacRae.

Mrs. Bauer stepped forward before Amber or Ethel could answer. "I think it's perfectly plain what it means," she said. "It means that you are raising children whose hearts are in the right place, though perhaps their judgment is not yet of the best. Don't you agree, Mrs. Streicher?" She appealed to another woman, who looked blank for a moment, then nodded.

Amber's knees felt weak, and she covered up her wobble with a curtsy. "Thank you, ma'am," she said. "I told Ethel we could count on you."

"I'm glad I come up to expectation." Mrs. Bauer smiled. "Mrs. MacRae, why don't you take us to see this Schneider child?"

"Certainly." She plastered on a fake smile. "He should be in the nursery."

"Oh, please!" Ethel's voice was squeaky with terror. "Mrs. Prine slaps him, and he's scared to death of her. He'll do much better with Luella."

"Of course he will!" Jane Henderson spoke up now. "They've had Luella training him. He's no better than a monkey, really."

"He is not," said Amber. "Have somebody here take him out of the nursery, if you want. He'll do just as well." She hoped. "But you'll have to have one of the girls, because all he knows is the deaf alphabet that we all taught him; and only a few words in that."

"We'll certainly bear it in mind," said Mrs. Bauer.

Mrs. MacRae led the committee out, and everyone was quiet while the sound of their feet and voices trailed away. Then everything hit the fan.

Amber and Ethel were switched till it seemed Miss Devine's arms would drop off. The peach switch whistled through the air and landed with dull swats on the backs of Amber's calves. She had to bite her lip nearly in two to keep from crying out, though after a while her calves got numb. Ethel also did not cry out during her turn; in fact, she seemed to get less miserable and more stubborn-looking with each switch.

The rest of the class time was devoted to a lecture on the wickedness of ingratitude. Miss Devine went into a lot of detail about how Amber was a ringleader who had led Ethel to her destruction. Amber didn't think anyone listened. The smell of fried chicken was creeping in, unbearably good after a month of ham and corn bread, and she could barely think for hunger.

At last the lunch gong rang. Entering the dining hall, Ethel tugged Amber's sleeve and pointed. "Would you look at that?" The committee was already seated at Mrs. MacRae's table, and Grof, wide-eyed, clutched a bouquet in Mrs. Bauer's lap!

Mrs. Bauer motioned them over. Grof signed "Hello." Mrs. MacRae was flushed and frowning, Mrs. Bauer flushed and smiling grimly. "I'm sure you're anxious to know what the verdict is," Mrs. Bauer said. "We aren't doctors, so we can't really judge; but I'm taking him to someone who can."

"Thank you, ma'am," said Ethel, signing "Hello" back at Grof.

"Meantime"—Mrs. Bauer smiled forcefully, and Mrs. MacRae looked sour—"Mrs. MacRae has agreed to let me sit with y'all for luncheon, if it's quite agreeable with you."

"Oh, yes, ma'am!" said Amber. Now she could complain about the food, and the slapping, and—it was better than a petition! "Did you ever find your daughter?" she asked as they led Mrs. Bauer (and Grof; the seating arrangement was going out the window) to a seat.

Mrs. Bauer's smile flickered and died. "No. It's as if the earth had swallowed her up, and I keep thinking—but never mind. This food smells delicious. Do you always eat like this?"

It was the most memorable meal of her time at the orphanage; and, as it turned out, the last. The last thing Mrs. Bauer did, over Aunt Sally Manger's strawberry pie, was return to the subject of Ada. "I miss her for herself, and no one can take her place," she said, "but we must muddle on as best we can, and there's no denying I miss her in a different way when the little ones need looking after and she's not around to help. Would you like to assist me, Amber? Room and board and a nickel a week."

And live right next door to the well! Amber almost choked on her pie, trying to get out the words: "Yes, ma'am!"

"I'll go settle it with Mrs. MacRae, then. Thank you for

having me." She bowed to Ethel and Amber, patted Grof on the cheek, and left. Amber sat back, feeling dizzy.

"Oh, Amber!" Ethel gazed at her with a strange expression. "Room and board and a nickel a week!"

"This is excellent! I get out, Grof gets diagnosed properly, and the committee knows about the food—bodacious!"

"It is tip-top that you're hiring out," said Ethel, looking at her hands.

"Oh, don't look like that." Amber felt a twinge of guilt. "I'd take you out too, if I could. But you've got to stay here to look after Grof. And things." Something her mom had said, about victory being sweet but short, passed through the back of her head. "Somebody's got to keep on them, you know. Miss Devine and Mrs. Prine aren't going to let any committee boss them around. You kids need a ringleader, or nothing'll get done."

Ethel swallowed, wiping Grof's chin. "I couldn't."

"Of course you could," said Amber stoutly. "Look how brave you turned out to be this morning."

"You think so?" Ethel looked uncertain, and Amber privately had her doubts, but it would do no good to voice them.

"I'm sure so," she said stoutly, scraping the plate for the last of the juice from the strawberry pie.

CHAPTER ELEVEN

Foster Home

During the last-day-of-school party in math class Ada and Violet sat in the back of their classroom discussing Violet's placement. "I've heard of these folks," Violet said. "They're in it for the money."

"Perhaps if you spoke to Mrs. Burak, she could find someone else for you," Ada suggested.

"Naw. I'm fine. I don't want to take a good spot away from some kid with problems."

Ada ducked to let an intricately folded paper construct fly over her head. "Vi," she said carefully, "if you don't have problems, why do you live—like this?"

"I didn't say my family didn't have problems," said Violet, catching the paper airplane and returning it to its sender with an expert flick of her wrist. "I mean I personally don't have the kinds of problems that need grownups to take care of them, like being retarded, or alcoholic, or like that."

"Oh," said Ada, and tried to think of a way to find out what the problems were without asking any personal questions. She couldn't. "I hope my placement is close enough so we can visit."

"Hey, we'll visit," said Violet, tearing a page out of her binder and beginning to fold her own paper airplane. "What we do, see—almost all the bus lines come downtown, so we can meet each other at the Alamo or somewhere. You know, the best thing"—she pinched the nose of her plane carefully into shape—"would be if you go to Streicher."

"Mrs. Burak said I would do best in a foster home."

"Mrs. Burak may not have a choice." Violet tested the plane for balance.

Ada's stomach hurt. She watched the airplane sail across the room and out the door. "How do you make those things work?" she asked abruptly.

In English they played word games; in Spanish, bilingual bingo. During art Ada took her work to the window to catch the sunlight (the fluorescent lights made her head ache) and saw Violet's PE class lining up for various track activities. She looked to see what Violet was doing, and found her by the fence, talking to a man. At this distance, she couldn't tell anything about him, except that he was also black, and that Violet talked to him for a long time. Violet did not mention him when they met next, and was distracted and silent the rest of the day.

Miss Capshaw stopped Ada after school as she went upstairs to change. "Ms. Burak called," she said. "Get a suitcase from the Goodwill and pack; she'll pick you up tomorrow at ten, when she comes for Vi."

Ada's heart thumped. "Where am I going?"

Miss Capshaw shrugged and walked toward the office. "Didn't say. Don't worry, she's a real fussy placer."

Ada trailed slowly upstairs, where the floor vibrated in a fixed rhythm—the boy down the hall with the boom box had turned it on already. Violet had pulled her own suitcase out of the top of the closet.

"Mrs. Burak's carrying me to my foster home tomorrow, too," said Ada. "Miss Capshaw didn't know where it would be."

Violet looked surprised. "That's funny. You usually get more warning than that. I bet Loyce's thrilled. A whole room doesn't open up at once very often!"

Ada sat on the bed. "Maybe we're going to the same house. That would be daisy."

"Uh, yeah." Violet carefully folded her underthings.

"Was that your father you were speaking with during PE?"

Violet jumped. "If you tell anybody, I'll skin you alive!"

"I won't," said Ada, "but I won't've been the only one who saw you. What's so terrible about speaking to your own father?"

"Nothing, if the world worked right, but it doesn't, so—look, you swear not to tell anybody if I explain some of it?"

"Honor bright," said Ada.

Violet tumbled the rest of her underwear willy-nilly into the suitcase. "I'm not going to that foster home tomorrow."

"You're going with your father instead? Why, that's—that's utterly daisy!"

"It'd be even daisier if I could stay with him." Violet stuffed her socks into pockets around the inside of the case.

"Why can't you?"

"Um—could we skip the why right now?" Violet tugged

138

her left braid and regarded Ada apologetically. "If I tell you why, I have to tell you stuff about . . . other people . . . too. If it were just my secrets, I'd tell you. For sure."

"Of course," said Ada, hiding an inward sigh.

"Okay. We'll get up tomorrow just like a regular Saturday, but instead of watching cartoons, I'll say I got to come up and pack. Only I'll already be packed. I'll get out the side door nobody uses and meet my dad at a place we set up today, and for a couple of weeks I'll just be gone. It's real important nobody finds out I'm with my dad."

"I won't tell. He's not—not a fugitive, is he?"

Violet frowned. "No more'n I am. Only—the way things are set up, he could get brought in for kidnapping me. It'd mess up everything we've been trying to do. That's not just him and me, either, it's Mom and Rosesharon. We're not doing anything wrong, but we're not doing everything legal. Get it?"

"You mean civil disobedience? Like Dr. Martin Luther King?" History class had dealt with civil rights the last week of school. To Violet and the history teachers, Dr. King was a bigger hero than George Washington.

Violet smiled. "I hope so. I don't know what he'd think of it. Anyway, if we messed up now I don't know how we'd fix it."

Ada's stomach was tying itself in knots. "Mrs. Burak knows something odd is going on with you," she said. "She says the system will catch you out."

Violet pushed her box of eye paint in between her T-shirts and shorts. "That's what my dad says, too. He says it's almost time we blew town."

Ada gulped.

Violet closed the suitcase. "Oh, don't look like that. I'm

going to try a new dodge, should get me through the summer, and you can be on your own a couple weeks, can't you? After that, we can meet downtown."

Ada relaxed. "Certainly I can. Only, it's such a comfort, having someone to be truthful with."

"Yeah, well, I wouldn't know." Violet tucked the suitcase under the bed.

Ada and Violet were resolutely normal all evening, though Ada felt like a bundle of nerves. She hardly slept at all that night, and in the morning Violet had to bounce on her bed to wake her.

"Wish I knew where you were going," said Violet softly as they ate their raisin bran. "I could call you when I get back. Give me a couple days to track you down, okay?"

Ada nodded. "What's a foster home like?"

"Oh—depends. Sometimes it's crowded, and sometimes you're the only kid there. You just got to roll with the punches." Violet picked a raisin out from between her front teeth. "It's probably a good thing I'm going away for a while. It'll give you a chance to get on your own feet. Time I get back, you won't even need me."

"Yes I will," said Ada.

After breakfast Violet clattered upstairs, calling to the world in general: "I got to go pack before Ms. Burak gets here! See you, Ada!"

"See you!" It wasn't much of a good-bye; but she must act as if she didn't know good-byes were necessary. Ada went into the dayroom where the children watched the Teenage Mutant Ninja Turtles. She wondered, idly standing dominoes in a pattern on one of the low tables, whether Toby and Doris would be as fascinated by these turtles as the twentieth-century children were. She wondered, tapping the first domino so that it fell onto the second and all fell in a chain, how Odett had done on her exams, without Ada to help her study.

Mrs. Burak arrived during the commercial preceding Bugs Bunny, and Ada went to greet her in the hall. The social worker wore a divided skirt and a resolutely cheerful expression; but the paint (Violet laughed at her for calling the makeup paint) she had used did not cover the bags below her eyes. "All set?" she asked brightly. "Where's Vi?"

"She went upstairs," said Ada. "I'll get her." She hurried upstairs, opened the door to her room, and wondered how she would act if she had not been forewarned. She picked up her suitcase, went to the girls' bathroom, and knocked. "Violet?" Her voice sounded false to herself. "Mrs. Burak's here."

"I'm not Violet," said whoever was inside.

"She's not up here," Ada said to Mrs. Burak, who had come halfway up the stairs. "Perhaps she went outside."

"What a time to disappear," grumbled Miss Capshaw.

"Disappear," said Mrs. Burak, wincing. "Oh, not again!"

"She was at breakfast this morning," said Miss Capshaw. "She can't have run off. Somebody'd have seen her."

Ada participated in the search, but it was hard to do so properly. Mrs. Burak couldn't seem to make up her mind whether to be amused or angry. When Miss Capshaw remembered the side door, which was always locked on the outside but always open from the inside, Mrs. Burak came down on the side of amusement. "She's outsmarted us again, Loyce," she said. "We'd better get used to it, and find a good place to hide the report."

"Why, that little . . ." Miss Capshaw looked positively fierce. "Who does she think she is?"

"I think she's doing her level best not to be anybody," said Mrs. Burak. "Where's your suitcase, Ada? You won't melt away on me, will you?"

"No, ma'am," said Ada. "My bag is by the door."

The car parked at the curb was smaller than the one in which the Buraks had driven her to the shelter, silver outside and red inside, where the red could be seen under dust and general untidiness. Ada put her bag in the cramped backseat, leaning against a box of old toys, and on top of a miscellaneous lot of paper trash. Mrs. Burak started the car, and the air conditioning and radio came on at the same time as the engine. The radio talked about current events, discussing countries Ada had never heard of. "Who will I be staying with?" she asked.

"Me," said Mrs. Burak. "Or, if you'd rather, I could take you to the folks who were going to foster Violet. But I pulled so many strings to get you into my house, it'll be a bit of a letdown if you don't come."

"Truly?" Ada was surprised at her own relief.

"Truly. But you don't have to come if you don't like."

"But I would *like* to stay with you. Tip-top!" An uncomfortable thought struck her. "But it won't make any difference to the things I've promised not to tell."

"That's fine, as long as you don't tell me any lies."

Ada hunched her shoulders. "I already have. In a fashion."

"You knew Vi was leaving?"

"Yes, ma'am."

"You know Vi could get in serious trouble, playing fast and loose with people the way she does?"

"Yes, ma'am. But I won't make it any better by telling on her." Thank goodness, Mrs. Burak didn't sound angry! "She didn't tell me much, but she promised me she wasn't doing anything wrong."

"Just against the rules." Mrs. Burak sounded amused again. "Well, I can hardly complain about that! I'm not exactly inside the rules this time, myself."

"You aren't?"

She shook her head. "I'm a social worker, not a foster parent. Dr. Cunningham'd say I was trying to sucker you into filling Amber's place. But there wasn't any good place to put you. And I'm interested in your case. And"—she shrugged—"the house is awfully empty without Amber in it."

Ada felt small and guilty. "I'm sorry about Amber."

"Oh, I haven't given up on her," said Mrs. Burak, with grim cheerfulness, as she mounted the ramp to the highway. "And don't worry, if she shows up tomorrow, I won't kick you out. And now we come to a decision point. Do you want to go to the house first, or do you want to go shopping?"

"Shopping?"

"I don't want Amber coming back and finding that I've given all her clothes away to some kid she's never met, and I don't want to dress you in hand-me-downs, either. So I'm taking you to the mall to get you some clothes of your own."

Ada's bag was filled with shabby cast-off frocks and

limp underthings. "Please, ma'am, let's go shopping first!"

Mrs. Burak laughed. "The mall it is!"

The mall was as long as ten city blocks and taller than the high school Matilda and Simpson attended. One could go from Dillard's at one end to Foley's at the other, and never see the sun. The air smelled stuffy, and the potted trees had no flowers, birds, or bees to enliven their branches. Ada had often heard the girls at school talk about meeting to "hang out at the mall." She could not understand why they preferred this place to a park, or to one another's homes.

However, the mall was wonderfully clean; and the stores were breathtaking. Ada could not look in any direction without seeing something new and wonderful. Ready-made clothes were everywhere, as well as stores devoted to selling candy, music machines and recorded music, furniture, toys, and things she had no name for.

Ada avoided the drugstore, for fear it would make her miss Pappa too much (not that the long white aisles resembled Pappa's dim, scented shop). She stopped at the toy shop window. It held so many wonderful toys. "I wish Odett were here." She sighed, involuntarily, gazing at the row of dolls in the costumes of all nations.

"Who's Odett?" asked Mrs. Burak casually, her eyes on the portrait dolls of famous actors of whom Ada had never heard.

"My little sister," said Ada.

"Maybe there's a way to bring her here without breaking your promises," suggested Mrs. Burak.

Ada shook her head. "Odett's with Mamma and

Pappa," she said, knowing that Mrs. Burak would take that to mean that she was dead. Which was—her stomach turned over—absolutely true. Odett, Matilda, Simpson—even Doris and little Toby—were dead of old age. She turned away from the toy store and walked quickly down the central aisle.

Mrs. Burak believed in shorts, sleeveless shirts, and low shoes made entirely of straps like a Mexican peon's ("sandals," she called them, though they did not resemble what Ada thought of as sandals). Ada, though she had grown accustomed to seeing reformed dress on others, could not bring herself to go half-naked in public, and used the religious argument suggested by Violet as a reason to buy only dresses. In August she would be a young lady of thirteen, old enough for skirts to her ankles, but in the meantime knee-length was quite suitable. As for sleeves—if no one else thought her bare arms indecent, she assured herself, it didn't matter whether they showed.

Mrs. Burak treated her to lunch in a cluster of restaurants on the mall's second story, and Ada decided to try pizza, which headed the list of dream foods for the children at the shelter. She found it untidy, but tasty. The afternoon was half gone before they stuffed their purchases in the "trunk" in the back of the car, and started for the Burak residence.

"I have no idea what your own home was like, of course," said Mrs. Burak as they drove through an area of low, long houses. "If you don't like our house, don't be afraid to tell me. My husband and I are sort of separated. He's taken a job in Austin and only comes down on weekends. We're considering a divorce." She took a deep breath. "I think that may have had something to do with Amber leaving. Dr. Cunningham gossiped to her, when we had—well, I had, it was my idea—put off telling her how we'd arranged things until after Fiesta so as not to spoil it for her. We meant to have a talk with her, the day after Battle of Flowers." She shook her head, trying to smile. "So I'm not infallible. Big shock. When she heard it from Dr. Cunningham, she probably thought we'd decided to divorce and—anyway, none of that is anything for you to worry about. My husband'll be in town this weekend till Monday afternoon, for Memorial Day."

Ada had not understood all of this, not having any idea of what a divorce was, but she nodded, hoping Mrs. Burak had a dictionary in her home.

"You can call us Lyle and Grace, or Aunt and Uncle, or whatever you're comfortable with. My husband's father lives down the street, and you'd better call him Mr. Burak." Her eyes flicked sideways at Ada. "Don't get upset if he picks on your name. He was thirteen years old when he and his mother escaped from Poland after the Nazis invaded. All the rest of his family died in camps. That makes him feel entitled to carry a grudge."

"But"—Ada hesitated only slightly, having become adept at hiding her ignorance—"I've nothing to do with knotsies."

"Oh, I know, honey! And he'll get past it, he's not a bigot. I'll take you to meet him tomorrow." Mrs. Burak pulled onto a concrete drive in front of a house made partly of slate-colored brick and partly of gray-painted wood. The car which had taken Ada to the shelter sat in the street. Ada opened the door on her side of the car and smelled fresh-cut grass. A grackle called in a hackberry tree.

146

Mr. Burak met them at the door, greeting Ada cordially. The front door opened into a carpeted room rather like the dayroom at the shelter, smaller and lacking the low tables. The ceiling hung low, and a film of dust dulled the furniture. "How'd you like the mall?" asked Mr. Burak, taking her suitcase.

"Very much, sir," said Ada, "but it made me giddy."

The bedroom where Ada would be staying overlooked the green and weedy backyard. Neater and more cheerful than the rest of the house, its narrow beds were covered in yellow chenille and stuffed animals. The curtains were also yellow, and the desk, bookcase, and bureau were white with gold trim. Mrs. Burak helped her unpack the shopping bags into a closet where Amber's clothes had been zipped up in a square bag to keep them out of the way. They didn't unpack the suitcase, to Ada's relief; Amber's hair ribbon was in it. When Violet came back, she would have to take charge of that ribbon.

Ada's gratitude could not keep her from noticing that the house was not truly comfortable. The space was too full, the air too stale, and the Buraks were too nervous. She listened attentively as they showed her how to use the equipment in the entertainment center and the kitchen and explained how her life would be arranged.

Mr. Burak was particularly careful to make sure that she understood the financial arrangements. "We're putting all the money the state will give us for fostering you into an account for your expenses," he said, showing her a ledger. "As far as we're concerned, that's your money." So far all the ledger held was a column of numbers in red, which he was copying off the receipts for her clothes. The amounts made Ada feel sick. She hadn't meant to be so expensive!

"If Grace takes you out to dinner and forgets to write it down, remind her."

"Oh, come on, Lyle," said Mrs. Burak. "You're such a nitpicker. Nobody has the time to audit our books."

"Will you get in bad trouble for taking me in?" asked Ada.

"No, no, don't worry about it." Mrs. Burak seemed to push the matter away with both hands. "The rules are a mess, and there's nobody to enforce them."

"Yet," said Mr. Burak.

"There won't be, either." She sounded exactly like Mamma did, when she and Pappa went over an old argument. "The more the government tries to fix the mess, the worse it gets. The only good any of us can do is on the human level."

"That attitude leaves an awful lot of people in the lurch," said Mr. Burak, sounding like Pappa in the same situation.

"I'm most grateful you didn't leave me there," said Ada, breaking in as she would have to distract her own parents. "May I use the calculator if I always put it back in the drawer?" She had seen people at school using these elegant little arithmetic machines, and longed to possess one.

After informing her of the house rules—absurdly lenient ones for the most part—they took her for a drive around the neighborhood. Ada would have preferred a walk, but did not like to say so. They showed her the bus stop where she could catch the number fifteen; the nearest swimming pool, convenience store, park, churches, and shopping centers. No children played in the yards, no dogs ran loose; she didn't even see any butterflies.

"You can borrow Amber's bike any time you want," said Mrs. Burak as they drove around, "but make sure you lock it securely any time you leave it. Don't just lock the front wheel, either; we've got bicycle thieves around here that detach the frame."

Ada's heart thumped. "I—I don't know how to ride a bicycle, ma'am," she said, "but I would very much like to learn."

"You don't know how?" Mr. Burak turned around and stared as if she had dropped from the moon. "I don't know what the world's coming to. Take us home, Grace; Ada and I have serious business to attend to."

Amber's bike was similar to a safety bicycle, but it also had gears to ease pedaling uphill, and hand-operated brakes. At first it was frightening, to be up so high and connected to the ground only by two tiny patches of rubber, but the opportunity was not one to be missed. She wished Billy Streicher could have seen her the first time she rode the length of the block!

By then she was hungry, and Mrs. Burak suggested they eat out, so they got into the car again (Mr. Burak's, this time) and went for Mexican food. After this they stopped at a video rental store, where Ada had the honor and responsibility of choosing what they would watch that evening. Bewildered by the thousands of mysterious choices, she seized upon the first familiar title she saw, and they returned to watch an overwhelmingly beautiful animation of the story of Sleeping Beauty. Neither the dull chewiness of the microwave popcorn Mr. Burak prepared, nor the low-voiced remarks the grown-ups made during the show, could dull her enjoyment.

"I know this is a sexist story, but you can't help loving this movie."

"What's sexist? Those fairies are the greatest role model little old ladies ever had."

"Yeah, but Briar Rose is such a wimp."

"Look at Ada. You'd think she'd never seen it before."

Ada said nothing, gazing at the screen with all her eyes. By the time the movie finished, she was too dazzled to face the polite difficulties of conversation with the Buraks. She excused herself to bathe and get ready for bed.

The bath restored Ada somewhat to the real world. She opened a window to air the bedroom, and turned on the desk lamp to study Amber's books. The bottom shelf was filled by a World Book encyclopedia, a dictionary, and a thesaurus. Remembering that she had meant to look up some words, she pulled out the dictionary. What was that first word? *D*-something. *Divorce*. "The dissolution of a marriage by law, or in primitive societies, by established custom."

Dissolution. She knew that word. It came from *dissolve*. Mr. and Mrs. Burak were considering not being married anymore? But—why? Just because he had found a good job in Austin? That made no sense. They seemed to like each other.

Not wanting to think about it, Ada paged on to the *KN*s and then the *N*s. The definition of *Nazi* was not useful, since she had never heard of the National Socialist party, so she tried the World Book. This was more detailed, but she almost wished it wasn't. Millions of people poisoned and burned to ashes or worked to death as slaves, flying machines pouring fire onto the great cities of Europe—she slammed the book shut, trembling. Germany had done all that? But—Germans were jolly and hard-working and had refused to own slaves before the War—Mamma and Pappa's war, between the states—Germans were . . . *She* was German. She felt as if a part of her had been mauled.

Shoving the *H* (for *Hitler* and *Holocaust*) volume back into its place, Ada scanned the titles on the upper shelves. Alcott and Dodge, Dickens and Lewis Carroll, dear *Black Beauty*, and a host of people she did not recognize, assured her that her mind need not dwell on horrors.

In the end, deciding that there was no friend like an old friend, she chose *Little Women* and took it to bed, turning off her reading light at the incredibly late hour of eleven. Then, realizing that she had forgotten to say her prayers, she slipped out of bed and knelt with her forehead pressed to the mattress.

"Our Heavenly Father," she whispered, and stopped. Something about Violet's presence had made her shy of praying properly at the shelter. She ought to make a better effort, now that she was all alone with the Holy Spirit. How did her present situation look from a heavenly point of view? Was Odett just as alive now as Violet, to Him, and the dangers of a Nazi-pursued Jew as urgent as those of a lost Amber? If one could move from one time to another, wouldn't all times be the same to God?

She rather thought they would, so she prayed to bless them all, her sisters and brothers a hundred years ago and Violet in whatever haven rejoined her to her father, and she prayed for Amber's safe return as well as for her own. Then she climbed into bed and lay, listening, for the first time in her life not hearing the breathing of another person in the room.

CHAPTER TWELVE

Little Orphant Amber

Amber loved her job at the Bauers' for a full quarter of an hour, at the end of which time Toby began crying furiously at not being allowed to eat dirt, and Doris chased her ball into the street, directly into the path of an oncoming wagon.

The Bauer house was everything she had always wanted—open and airy, with large rooms, porches, wallpaper, lace curtains, and canopies on almost all the beds. Her complete private space, however, was a cot between Toby's and Doris's cribs, with a small chest for her clothes. She lay awake at night, recalling her bookshelves, her bunk beds set side by side, her stuffed animals. When I get back, she promised herself, I'll never complain that room's too small again!

Amber soon figured out that Odett had spent most of her life tagging after the missing Ada, and didn't know what to do with herself on her own. Oh, sometimes she went next door and played with the Streichers, but mostly, if Amber gave the kids a bath, she hung around asking to help; or if Amber took the kids into the backyard, Odett hung around asking if they wanted to play with her rag dolls. Sometimes she was a help; other times she was a pain, especially when she started talking about Ada.

Ada always let them climb the fence and jump off. Ada treated them to candy and tamales. Ada could make wonderful doll clothes, and paper dolls, and jump clear across the flower beds, and didn't pull hair when she combed it, and had no freckles. Some of this Amber believed like she believed the world was flat. Some of it made her feel how unsuited she was to looking after small children without the aid of TVs and video games. Some of it just totally bored her.

One day Doris's battered rag and wax babies acted as tea hostesses to Toby's much-chewed rubber-headed doll and Odett's china-headed family, with Amber waiting on table and hauling the teapot back and forth as instructed. At least it kept their clothes clean. "We should have flowers on the table," declared Doris, turning toward the beds at the side of the house. "I will pick some."

"Not those flowers," said Amber. "Um—they're not ripe."

"Flowers don't get ripe!" said Doris witheringly.

"They do, too," said Amber, having already learned that it was useless to try to reason with Doris. She spotted blooming huisache and dwarf sunflowers in the Haunted Lot. "Look, there's some yellow ones, to match the flowers on the teapot."

"We can't go into the Haunted Lot," said Odett. "The ghosts'll get us. Like Ada."

"Bull," said Amber. "Don't scare the little kids. We

don't have to go into the lot for flowers, just stand on the edge. And there aren't any ghosts."

"Are too," declared Toby, looking like a little girl in his skirts and shoulder-length hair. "They laugh at me."

"And they took Ada." Doris's voice changed, as it did when she was working herself up to cry. "I want Ada back!"

"Of course you do," said Amber. "And you'll get her back, because there aren't any ghosts in this lot. Look at this!" She grabbed a bushy shrub whose flowers had centers the size of the silver dollars with which Mrs. Bauer paid delivery boys. "This is a sunflower! Ghosts don't hang around in the sun, do they? Why should they hide in the sunflowers, then?"

A hollow moan sounded from the shadows of the shrubs. Odett, Toby, and Doris fell back with cries of terror.

"Get out of there, Billy!" ordered Amber, impatiently. "Stop scaring the kids and be useful. You got your knife?"

The boy from next door—the same boy she had met on Nolan Street that first day—crawled out and brushed off his short pants, followed by a cloud of varicolored butterflies. "Always ready to assist a damsel in distress!" he declared, whipping out his bone-handled pocketknife and flipping the blade open.

The kids relaxed. Everybody on the block seemed to think Billy Streicher was the coolest thing that ever walked the earth. Amber disliked cool dudes on principle, but at least he gave them something to think about besides ghosts. She held out her hand for the knife. "Thanks. I was just making a centerpiece."

"Allow me." He began cutting sunflower blossoms.

"What for? I can cut as well as you can."

"But it's my knife. What've we got to put them in?"

"I'll get the bowl!" Odett ran back to the tea party.

"What's this 'we' business?" asked Amber. "You taking up doll tea parties?"

"I'm only being helpful. Great Caesar's ghost, you're as prickly as Ada!"

"See, he believes in ghosts," said Toby.

"Don't start them up again," moaned Amber.

"*Great Caesar's ghost* is just an expression," Billy assured Toby. "You don't have to worry about him coming after you."

"Ghosts took Ada," said Doris stubbornly.

"Ada ran off because she was tired of minding y'all," said Billy, "and I don't blame her. If I didn't have such a weighty responsibility as only son, I'd leave my little sisters, too."

"Ada wouldn't run off!" protested Odett, returning with the chipped bowl that had been holding invisible sugar. "And she did go to the Haunted Lot. I saw her out of the window."

"And then the ghost got her," declared Doris. "It tried to get Toby before, pretending to be a doggy, and then it got Ada."

"Just because nobody saw her leave the lot doesn't mean she didn't," said Billy, dumping the sunflowers into the bowl. He turned to Amber and grinned wickedly. "They found you in the Haunted Lot the same day, didn't they? Maybe it was a trade."

"Yeah, right. Little Orphant Amber for Big Sister Ada," said Amber, not caring whether he caught the reference to the "Little Orphant Annie" poem (which might or might

155

not be around yet). "Thanks for the flowers. Are you going to bring your dolls and play, or are you going now?"

That sent him off toward the street, whistling, and not nearly as insulted as he should have been. As they re-arranged the tea party to suit Doris's taste, Odett looked at Amber with an odd expression. "Ada didn't like Billy, either."

"Ada had good taste," said Amber, trying to crush the ants out of the "cookie" tray, which was full of buttons borrowed from the jar in the mending basket.

"You look like Ada, some," said Odett, "but you're not like her, really."

"Well, you wouldn't want me to be, would you?" Amber asked absently. She barely heard what Odett answered. Ada—vanished into the Haunted Lot carrying a piece of brown sugar candy, on the same day Amber had appeared carrying a purse full of atomic fireballs. Was there some connection?

At this point, Toby spilled the buttons, Doris slapped him, and all possibility of thought fled till dinnertime. It was always like this anymore. Even when Doris and Toby went down for their naps, Frieda or Mrs. Bauer were just as likely to have some chore or errand for Amber. Frieda seldom left the kitchen, she was so busy producing meals which, delicious as they were, did not seem to Amber to be worth all the work she put into them. The wood stove was never allowed to go out because it was such a pain to relight, so Frieda was always red-faced and sweating, and Amber didn't have the heart to refuse to stir a saucepan for her while she labored at the water pump. The only time Frieda got any rest was Sunday, when she popped a roast into the oven in the morning before church and then left to spend the rest of the day with her sister's family.

Amber didn't like to refuse Mrs. Bauer, either. After all, she was the boss, and she was as busy as Frieda, cleaning the house, sewing, or dressing up to go to meetings of the Women's Christian Temperance Union or the Suffragist Association of San Antonio. A lot of the errands she wanted done seemed to Amber to be a lot of walking for nothing, though; and too many involved Odett. "Amber, run down to Wolff and Marx for some pins, and take Odett to pick out that new ribbon for her hat." Stuff like that. Wolff and Marx's store was clear downtown, no distance at all by car, but farther than she'd ever normally have walked.

"I wish we had a streetcar closer," grumbled Odett one day.

"I wish we had bikes," Amber said, walking with Odett and Pinkie and Dot Streicher over the plank bridge across the Alamo Ditch. This was a little piece of the river, used to irrigate gardens; the water in it was high and brown after the wet spring and dotted with floating trash. "This trip'd be nothing."

"We've got a bicycle," said Dot, "but you couldn't ride it."

"I could, too," said Amber. She could feel her feet swelling inside these stupid tight boots. "I've ridden bikes before."

"Oh, you liar!" Pinkie stamped her feet to make the bridge shake. "Nobody'd let you ride a bicycle!"

"Why not?" Amber pushed her glasses up her nose.

"Ladies don't ride bicycles," said Dot primly.

"I bet your brother told you that," said Amber, stretching her arm out like a school-crossing guard so no one would run into the street in front of the brewery wagon.

"Ladies don't bet, either." Pinkie's nose was so high in the air it was a wonder she could see in front of her.

"Seems to me women who worry about being ladies don't get to do much," said Amber, leading the sprint across the road. She hated crossing without lights or stop signs or even lanes of traffic! To her satisfaction, Pinkie tripped on the curb and tore a hole in her stocking.

Next afternoon, when Amber and Odett were teaching Toby and Doris hopscotch, Billy and a small knot of hangers-on strolled up. In addition to his younger sisters, the group included the boys who had teased Amber that first day and other neighborhood children, girls and boys. They all hung back in the street while Billy leaned against the chinaberry tree and watched Toby successfully pick up the button marker from the middle of the pattern Amber had scratched in the street dust.

"Good afternoon, Little Orphant Amber," Billy said.

"Hi," said Amber. "Hey, Toby, you're getting good at this!"

"Pinkie says you say you can ride a bicycle," Billy said.

"I can," said Amber. "So what?"

"So that's hard to believe."

Amber shrugged. "Whether you believe it or not won't change anything. C'mon, Toby, it's Doris's turn."

Toby reluctantly turned the button over to his sister and leaned against Amber's legs to watch.

"What kind of bicycle?"

"An ordinary bicycle," said Amber. "What's your problem?"

158

"So if I showed you my father's bicycle, you could ride it."

"Of course I could. Anybody can ride a bike."

"Let's see you do it, then. I dare you."

"Fine. You've dared me. When the kids are done playing—"

"We're done!" said Doris, breathlessly.

Amber shrugged and followed Billy, Doris and Toby trotting beside her and every kid in the neighborhood trailing after. There must be some catch, or everybody wouldn't be so interested.

The carriage house was dim and dusty, smelling pleasantly of hay and horse. The Streichers' speckled ("flea-bitten") gray horse watched over the door of her stall as they filed past the carriage, and Billy picked up the bicycle from the rear wall.

Amber's heart sank. Its front wheel was almost as tall as she was, and its rear no bigger than a pie plate. She'd seen a picture of this once, and Mom had told her what it was.

"That's not an ordinary bicycle. That's a pennyfarthing."

"Of course it's an ordinary," said Billy. "Pappa bought it before safeties were invented."

"I knew she was lying," muttered someone in the crowd.

"She was not!" said Odett unexpectedly. "You can ride it—can't you, Amber?"

Amber looked at the encircling faces and saw she had no choice. "It's taller than the one I rode before," she said, "but if I can reach the pedals, I'll give it a shot."

The contraption towered above the clustered children

159

as it was pushed out into the carriage yard, and Amber had to climb onto the ornamental block by the door to get as high as the seat. She hesitated before mounting, remembering her responsibilities. "Y'all keep out of my way," she ordered, "and Odett, you keep a tight hold of Doris and Toby." When she saw Odett obey, she grasped the handlebars, stepped on the near pedal, swung her leg over the tiny seat, and set off.

The wheel was too tall for her, so that she nearly lost the pedal at the lowest part of the turn. The machine wobbled down the carriage drive, and she thought it was going to fall as she turned onto the street, but she kept her balance and started to pick up speed. The children ran after her, cheering. The height was scary, and the hard rubber tires exaggerated the shock of every bump in the road. The children cheered louder as she went faster, going through the intersection and then turning the bike in a broad loop across the street. Dogs ran after her, barking, and women came out on their porches.

Mrs. Bauer ran out, too, and a laundry wagon was about to cross her path. She'd better get back to her job. Amber shoved down on the pedal, and kept going.

What the—? This bike had no brakes! She jerked the handlebars to whizz past the rear of the laundry wagon, picking up speed. Mr. Bauer was walking down the street on his way home, and stopped dead when he saw her. Amber turned the bike to slow herself—but if it slowed too much, she would fall off. She would have to jump while it was still moving.

Amber pulled her feet up, let the bike coast, and turned sideways. Too fast . . . too fast . . . slower . . . now, or she'd lose her nerve. She jumped, landed, felt a sharp pain in her ankle, and tried to catch the bike; but Mr. Bauer had already caught it.

"Whew! Thanks, sir." Amber straightened.

"What's the meaning of this?" he asked sternly.

The other children, even Odett, stepped back, except for Billy. "It's my doing, sir. I dared her."

Odett still clung to the wiggling Doris and Toby. "They called her a liar, Pappa."

"He also didn't tell me it didn't have brakes," said Amber.

"Of course it doesn't," said Billy, as if she had complained that it didn't have leather upholstery and a snack bar. "She rode it utterly tip-top, sir, except for the flying dismount." He looked at her with respect.

Mr. Bauer looked at her with nothing of the sort. "Did you hurt yourself?"

"Twisted my ankle. You can let the kids go now, Odett."

Released, Doris and Toby seized their father's legs and gabbled. Mrs. Bauer ran up, and Dot cried: "Here comes Pappa!"

"Am I right in thinking you did not consult your father about this venture?" Mr. Bauer asked, as Billy cast an anxious glance at the figure approaching from downtown.

"You are, sir. I didn't think she'd take the dare."

Mr. Bauer gave his arm solemnly to Amber to help her limp to the porch. Amber was put on the sofa in the front room, her foot on a hassock and her boot removed, though it already didn't hurt as much. "You might have sprained your ankle," clucked Frieda.

Amber said nothing. If 1891 bikes didn't come with

brakes, she couldn't make any excuses that didn't sound dumb or whiny.

Toby climbed onto the sofa next to Amber and patted her knee. "Amber's daisy!"

"Don't you have anything to say, Amber?" asked Mrs. Bauer.

Amber considered her words carefully. Mr. Bauer still looked mad, but Mrs. Bauer seemed more pleased than otherwise. "I guess I shouldn't let Billy push me into doing things when I'm supposed to be watching the kids," she said, "but Odett hung on to them real good, and he's such a"—not jerk; nobody here knew what a jerk was—"he's really asking to be proved wrong all the time. So I'm sorry if I didn't do my job right and I'm sorry I borrowed Mr. Streicher's bike without permission, but I'm not sorry I showed Billy up this once. Next time he tries it, I'll remind him about this and tell him to buzz off."

"I don't think you can say fairer than that, Albrecht."

Mr. Bauer's eyes were like two blue marbles. "Do you consider that you have acted like a young lady, Amber?"

"She's not a young lady, Albrecht," said Mrs. Bauer sharply. "She's only a hired girl."

"A certain standard of decorum is required for all members of the sex, whether they be hired girls or queens."

"Required by whom?" asked Mrs. Bauer. "You can't expect a twelve-year-old to refuse a dare and retain self-respect!"

The Bauers seemed to have forgotten that their children were in the room, intent only on their argument. Amber shoved her foot back into her boot and asked Frieda, inspired by the smell of sauerbraten: "Is it almost dinnertime?"

The cook nodded. "You'd best get the children cleaned up."

So Amber hustled Doris, Toby, and Odett to the washroom, leaving the older Bauers to their argument. She wanted to go home more than anything.

That was the last day of high school. Simpson and Matilda came home burdened by books and papers, including some half-used copybooks which they donated to their younger sisters. Amber claimed one that had originally held chemistry notes and hid it under the mattress of her cot. After Mr. Bauer had led evening prayers (much simpler, easier-to-swallow ones than Mrs. MacRae's); after Matilda read aloud from the serial story in the newspaper while Amber and Mrs. Bauer and Frieda mended clothes; after everyone had gone to bed, Amber got up again.

The house was much darker than seemed natural, because there were no streetlights, and no glows from VCRs and microwaves and clock radios. With a borrowed candle and some matches from the kitchen, she made a little cave of light in one corner by opening the door of the armoire which served as a closet, and hiding behind it. In this narrow privacy she crouched, writing all the details she could gather about Ada's disappearance and all she could remember of her own. If she could only concentrate, put the right facts in the right order and make sense of them, she would be able to go home. She must be able to.

But she was too sleepy.

CHAPTER THIRTEEN

Standing Alone

Some things had been greatly improved during the century, Ada had to admit. The dentist Mrs. Burak took her to was completely painless, and when Mr. Burak took her to an eye specialist, he was able to fix her up with a pair of spectacles the same day. She chose round wire frames, which made her look a little owlish, but would arouse no wonder in her own time. The degree to which they improved her vision astonished her.

The worst difficulty was that she was almost always alone. The neighboring children played in their own backyards, and she did not know how to approach them. Mrs. Burak worked, and Mr. Burak was in Austin during the week. The only real acquaintance she had in this new neighborhood was Old Mr. Burak.

She didn't call him that to his face. She called him and Mr. Burak "sir," that unfailing standby. He was not as old as her grandfather, but had retired from his business a few weeks ago, in order, he said, to start up a new business before he got too old. He was a stocky man, who dressed exactly as other men dressed, not what Ada expected a Jew to look like at all. Bearing in mind what Mrs. Burak had said about him, Ada shook hands with him firmly when she was introduced, and did her best to put them on a solid footing at once.

"My grandparents came from Germany," she said, "but they had nothing to do with Nazis. I'm sorry about your relatives."

He raised his bushy eyebrows and smiled. "Grace's been warning you about me, hasn't she?"

Mrs. Burak turned red. "You do pounce on people, you know."

"Only doing my duty," said Old Mr. Burak. "Why'd your grandparents leave Germany, kid?"

Ada had decided to be truthful, but not detailed, on this point. "Opa and Oma wanted to live in a republic," she said, "plus they could make a better living here."

This seemed to please him, and he took her into his study to see his collections of stamps and coins. "I did these as a hobby," he said, "but my children don't care about them, so now I deal in them, and God willing they can keep me from starving in my old age." Ada was astonished at how much money an ordinary threepenny stamp could cost now. Whenever the lonesomeness overwhelmed her, she found that Old Mr. Burak was willing to show her how to grade and mount and price these odd valuables.

Photographs of Amber reproached Ada from on top of the TV, the stereo, the end tables—Amber at three, playing with a stuffed bear and wrinkling her nose at the camera; Amber at ten, sandwiched between her parents on a photographer's sofa; Amber at twelve-going-on-thirteen, freckled and showing no signs of vanishing. "We are connected," said the pictures, in Ada's head; "Find me, and we can both come home."

Ada had no idea how to go about looking, but Mrs. Burak bought her a bus pass, and Ada set out on her own into the bewildering city. She bought a map and marked it with colored pens (those delightful free-flowing pens that never needed ink!), noting again how huge the city had grown. The Buraks' house was farther north than she had ever been in her life, and the city continued another ten miles or so after that!

The number fifteen bus, which she took into downtown, went down the very street Pappa's drugstore had been on—then a moderately busy, prosperous place, lined with yellow-brick and limestone buildings, and more going up all the time. Now the street was forgotten in the shadow of the highway, Pappa's store gone without a trace, and buildings not yet built at the time of her departure crumbling with age. She would pass near the Streicher place, and that alien blue building where her own home had been, and look the other way, wondering what the strange creature that inhabited the well was doing, what it wanted.

Glum and at the end of her resources one day, Ada followed the concrete riverside walk that turned south at the main library, carrying an armload of books that she hoped, but did not believe, would give her a new idea. The walk led into an area she had known as the Little Rhein. In other parts of the city, buildings towered over the river; but the sky here was open and the sunny banks, though paved, were broad.

Suddenly, her heart thumped. She knew that house! She rode past it every time she visited Oma and Opa! And it looked just as it should, with its tin roof shining in the sun and its garden so neat! And there was the arsenal— and what's-his-name's house, with the natatorium where he held private swimming parties. She hurried up to street level.

Everything was as it ought to be, if she ignored the blacktop streets, the cars, the lack of children in the yards, and the occasional change in color scheme. These houses were still homes, not law offices and child-care centers! With her heart in her mouth, she hurried past the fancy houses where the rich Germans had lived, into the modest neighborhood of her grandparents. Here the houses were less imposing, and less universally well kept. She ran the last block and stopped in front of the house, its gallery, its keyhole-shaped doorway, and its wrought-iron fence.

Ada trembled and her breath came in short gasps. Oma's wild morning glory had been replaced by yellow roses. The house was cream-colored with brown trim, instead of white and green, and instead of a gravel walk someone had laid a concrete sidewalk, which had buckled. But no one had done anything to it that Oma and Opa might not have done, in the fullness of time. What if she opened this gate . . . walked up that walk . . . pushed that door. . . .

An old woman came out, carrying a broom. She wore a T-shirt that said LITTLE OLD LADY IN TENNIS SHOES. She looked at Ada, and asked: "You looking for somebody, honey?"

Ada began crying so suddenly she didn't realize she was

going to do it, and she couldn't stop, until the Little Old Lady in Tennis Shoes had made her sit down on the steps and brought her a glass of water. She was a sweet old lady, and Ada was able to suppress her tears the sooner, because she didn't like upsetting her. After cleaning her face with her handkerchief and getting her voice back under control, Ada could not help asking: "Do you know anything about some people named Bauer?"

The Little Old Lady in Tennis Shoes frowned thoughtfully. "Bauer. Now that's—yes, of course! The family that built this house was named Bauer. However did you know that?"

"How—how long did they live here?" gulped Ada.

"I'm not right sure. The family owned it till the forties, but the neighborhood was in a decline for a while and they may have rented it out. I bought it from a Mexican family ten years ago—or my husband did—and it really is the most delightful little house." She patted Ada's shoulder. "But those are the only Bauers I know anything about. What address have you got?"

"I don't—I—it's all right." Ada's mind was blank.

"If you say so," said the Little Old Lady doubtfully. "I know kids aren't allowed to take food from strangers, but I just made chocolate chip cookies. Will you take some if I eat, too?"

Ada nodded, and the Little Old Lady vanished, to return with a plate of pale brown cookies with dark brown spots, and two glasses of milk. Ada took a bite politely, and opened her eyes wide. This was a real cookie—not one of those hard things out of a bag in Mrs. Burak's pantry! And the milk was almost like real milk—a tad too cold, but thick, not the thin low-fat stuff she had been served ever since she came. It tasted so good she had to work not to seem greedy.

"I purely like to see a child enjoy her food," said the Little Old Lady with satisfaction.

"These are daisy!" said Ada, "I mean, excellent. My foster mother's kind, but she never bakes anything."

"Too busy, I expect," said the Little Old Lady. "Does she let you use the oven?"

"Only the microwave. It's a gas oven, and she doesn't want me around the open flame while she's gone."

"I don't blame her. Still, it's too bad. Microwaves are okay for things like melting chocolate, but not for baking."

"I hate them," said Ada. "The food doesn't smell right. And all I have to cook in it is packaged food and leftovers."

They had a pleasant conversation about cooking, so that Ada was able to go on her way feeling somewhat comforted, though aware of a deep ache inside that she had been ignoring for weeks.

She started to read the first book on the bus home, and found it promising, since it contained a creature who granted wishes. If she could talk to the thing in the well, as these children talked to the Psammead . . . but how to make it respond? It all seemed so hopeless! Desperately lonesome, she went to help Old Mr. Burak sort a collection of pennies he had just bought.

One wall of his study was covered with black-and-white photographs of people and places in Poland. The sight of the spires, and the stiff white faces, fit in well with Ada's melancholy. She and Old Mr. Burak listened to the public radio station, which today was talking mostly about Russian elections, and a volcanic eruption in the Philippines.

"Will you go back to Poland, now things are better over

169

there?" asked Ada, who had gathered that the government of Russia had cast a pall over all the countries on its borders since the war against the Nazis and that it was now lifting.

"What for?" asked Old Mr. Burak. "To see where my people were murdered?" He nodded at the wall of pictures. "That's all of Poland that mattered to me, and all of it's gone, except maybe some of the buildings. What good's a building without your people in it?"

That question hit too close for comfort. Ada bent over the bronze Indianhead pennies she was sorting by date. "What if you could go back to the people?" she asked. "Go back in time?"

"Now, there's an idea," said Old Mr. Burak. "Go back, smuggle them out—I'd like that. But it wouldn't work even if you had the time machine. Why would they listen to me? I'd be this old man from nowhere, telling them the Germans are going to kill six million of us. Sure, there've been pogroms, but six million people? In those days, nobody thought anything like that could be done, which is how the Nazis were able to do it." He inserted a penny into a display card and wrote "VF," for *Very Fine*, in the corner. "Besides, I can't hardly speak Polish and Yiddish anymore."

"You could see everyone again, though."

"They wouldn't know me. Seeing them would just hurt all over again. Listen." He tapped the table with a steel penny. "Grace and Lyle think something horrible must've happened with you. They say your whole family seems to be dead or run out on you or something, and they want you to talk about it. I don't want to hear what you've been through, I got enough of that of my own, thank you very much." He took off his spectacles, pulling out a handkerchief to polish them. "What I know is, talking doesn't change the past. Nothing changes the past. You learn from it, you live with it, and"—he pointed an earpiece at her—"you change the future. That's the important thing, that you make the future different from the horrible past."

"That's easy to say," said Ada. "Anyway, the past isn't all horrible. Parts of it are better than now."

Old Mr. Burak laughed and put his glasses back on. "You sound like Amber there," he said. "She was on this history kick. She hears Grace and Lyle talking about how bad things are now, and she reads these books about what it was like a hundred years ago, and she thinks life was better. And sure, some things were. But some things weren't; and, anyway, you take what you got. It's the people from a hundred years ago that stuck us with the way things are now, and whatever we do, the people a hundred years from now will be stuck with that."

Mrs. Burak got home late, as usual, and Ada helped her make a spaghetti supper. The canned sauce was fairly tasteless on its own, so Ada dug in the pantry for spices. All she found were minced garlic and onion powder, so she added them, and they helped some. "There's a recipe in the cookbook," she suggested, "that calls for oregano, and basil, and fresh tomatoes, and it doesn't sound hard. Don't you think we could try it sometime?"

"I don't know," said Mrs. Burak, shaking grated parmesan cheese over her serving. "You have to simmer spaghetti sauce forever. And spices are expensive."

"It would taste ever so much better, though," Ada pointed out, "and spices last a long time." She ate a bite.

She had heard that Italian cooking was supposed to be almost as good as French; but if this were a sample, she'd take German every day. It would not do to make Mrs. Burak feel she was ungrateful and demanding, however. "If you can't afford it, it doesn't matter," she said. "I don't want to be a burden on you."

"You're not a burden," said Mrs. Burak. "I hate coming home to an empty house."

"It must be hard, to be missing Amber, and your husband most of the time as well," said Ada, trying to sound grown-up.

"Actually, we're getting on better now that we only see each other on weekends," said Mrs. Burak. "I thought for a while we were going to have to get a divorce, but now—I don't know." She frowned at her spaghetti.

"I think people ought to stay married," declared Ada. "What's the use of promising 'till death do you part' if you don't mean it?"

"What's the use of pretending?" asked Mrs. Burak. "If we stayed together and all we did was fight, that would just be a different way of breaking our promise." She shook herself. "How did we get from spaghetti to this? I'll pick up some spices this weekend, if you remind me, but I don't promise to cook."

"I can follow a recipe," said Ada, who had helped Frieda in the kitchen once in a while, and liked it.

"Well . . . if I'm here to supervise, maybe."

After supper they rinsed all the dishes before putting them into the dishwashing machine. Ada thought they might as well wash them all outright, but this wasn't her house, so she let it go. They then sat down for a game called Scrabble while the TV ran in the background. The voice of the TV made the two of them seem less alone in the house, which to Ada always felt so empty.

That night she dreamed of Amber, going home with Violet, and falling into the well. When she landed with a splash at the bottom, Ada sat up. Beyond her open window, the rain poured, the sound of its fall muffled without a tin roof to ring against. Two weeks, she thought. I've had the freedom of the city, and what have I accomplished? Nothing, nothing, nothing! When the rain tapered off she lay down again, but did not sleep.

Next day she took the number fifteen bus early and got off near the Haunted Lot. It was a bright and muddy morning and the children on the play equipment in the Streichers' yard got dirty rapidly. Ada strolled by, averting her eyes from the blue warehouse, and slipped into the sunflowers of the Haunted Lot.

Within a few steps she was drenched from the wet plants, but in the June warmth this was not uncomfortable. When she got to the well, she knelt on the rim. "Hello, down there!"

"Air," echoed the well.

"It's me, Ada." The echoes ran so close behind her voice that only the last syllable did not overlap. "Please. I need something to go on."

"On."

This was not working. "What is it you're after?"

Grackles screeched, and water dripped from the huisache. Not far distant, a metallic rattle was followed by a rustle and a thump. Someone had climbed the fence.

The unknown forced his way through the wet brush.

Ada retreated behind the stump. She had as much right here as anyone—but what if this were someone dangerous? What if it were someone about to make a wish in the well? If she stayed, she might learn something. She twisted her hands nervously. If only Violet were here!

Violet's head popped out of the huisache.

Ada squealed and hurled herself upon her. "Vi!"

"Hey! Ada!" Violet rocked back in surprise, but, being Violet, recovered quickly. "I saw somebody come in here out of the window upstairs, so I figured I better check it out."

Something splashed, and both girls jumped. Someone had carved two curving arrows, each pointing to the blunt end of the other, into one of the encircling roots of the old stump. Violet pointed at it. "Was that there before?"

"No," said Ada. "I was trying to make—it—speak, but it wouldn't." She frowned. "I suppose that's my answer."

Violet snorted and leaned over the well. "Thanks a lot, you! That's clear as mud."

"It's my belief," said Ada, slowly, "that the poor thing can't speak, and can't be seen. Perhaps it's doing the best it can, already, and we simply aren't clever enough to work it out."

"The best it can do's pretty sorry, then." Violet sat on the edge of the well and crossed her legs in the unladylike way that all women did these days. "So where'd they put you?"

Amber sat down next to her. "With Mrs. Burak."

"I didn't know they'd let a social worker foster."

"She says she's done an 'end run' round the rules, whatever that means." Ada looked at Violet, wanting to ask a hundred things and say a hundred things, all at once. "I'm glad you're back," she said. "And isn't it lucky they placed you here?"

"Nope," said Violet, grinning like the Cheshire cat. "Not luck at all. I placed myself."

"How?" Without prompting, Ada crossed her heart.

"Oh, it was easy," Violet assured her. "There's one social worker who can't remember faces and names to save her life, and her paperwork's always a mess. I showed up on the doorstep yesterday with some placement paperwork I—got hold of—and filled out my own self, and said she'd sent me. They just shoved me into a bedroom and I'm set for a while."

Ada knew it was her duty to frown in disapproval, though she felt like doing anything in the world but frowning. "There's not much point in having rules, if people like you and Mrs. Burak go around breaking them."

"You can't break something that already ain't working." Violet grinned, and Ada was not in any mood to argue with her.

CHAPTER FOURTEEN

Stealing Time

"Oh, Amber!" called Mrs. Bauer, as Amber (having put Doris and Toby down for their naps) tiptoed toward the door. "Frieda's got a ferocious toothache. Could you run to Mr. Bauer's store and fetch some drops?"

Amber gritted her teeth and did not turn. "I don't know the way, ma'am."

"Take Odett. You may as well make a proper walk of it," Mrs. Bauer continued cheerfully, opening her purse. "Your nerves must be screaming to escape this house!" She smiled so kindly that Amber made herself smile back.

"Yes, ma'am," she said. "But yours must be, too. Why don't you go to the store and I'll help Matilda?" After she had paid her visit to the well, she promised herself.

Mrs. Bauer shook her head. "No, you run along."

So Amber accepted the money, collected Odett, tied them both into bonnets, and set out along the damp street. Though they were halfway through June, rain had fallen every few days, keeping the mosquitoes lively. Amber was constantly dabbing thick pink calamine lotion all over herself and her charges.

Odett trotted ahead, telling her whose father worked at what in which building. Amber nodded and made encouraging sounds, racking her brain for a plan to get into the Haunted Lot alone. Today had looked like a good chance, with Frieda lying in bed with her toothache, Matilda and Mrs. Bauer busy, and Simpson starting work at his father's store. Tomorrow she wouldn't even be in the area, because of the weekly Sunday outing. For the hundredth time she considered letting on that she was Jewish. Church with the Bauers was better than church with the orphans, but she felt like a coward, sitting through services; and it took up valuable time. The Bauers were so German, though, and Grandad had told her so many stories. . . .

Odett tugged at her hand. "There's El Dulcero! Have you got any money?"

"No," said Amber, shortly, "and if I did, I wouldn't spend it on you." She was fed up with everything.

"We could share. That's what Ada would have done."

"Pinkie says y'all used to call Ada a skinflint."

"Well—sometimes. But I didn't mean it, and I'm sorry."

"So don't give yourself something else to be sorry for by trying to con a poor, hardworking orphan out of her pitiful wages," said Amber. "If I got lost in the Haunted Lot next week, you'd feel awful guilty."

"Don't joke about it," said Odett, looking suddenly solemn. "It's utterly dreadful, what happened to Ada."

"You don't know what happened to Ada," said Amber.

"I do so," said Odett. "I have it all worked out. Something was trying to lead Toby into the Haunted Lot. Sooner or later it would have done it, too. That something must have gone after Ada."

"As far as I can tell, Toby tried to follow a dog into the Haunted Lot, and you're making up the rest," said Ada.

Odett folded her arms. "Billy sees lights in the lot most every night—only he's hardly seen them at all since Ada vanished. What do you say to that?"

"I say Billy's full of it—I mean, talking through his hat." Amber corrected her twentieth-century expression into one that Odett would understand. "Ada wasn't—isn't dumb enough to be lured to her doom like a three-year-old, is she?"

"No," said Odett, "but she was in charge of the little ones. I think"—she took a deep breath and looked so deadly serious Amber wanted to laugh—"she sacrificed herself to save Toby from this thing's evil clutches!"

Amber let herself laugh. "Don't you think if she found some kind of bogey-monster going after Toby, she'd have told somebody? There's no point telling grown-ups these things, but I'd get hold of you, and Pinkie—any of the kids that'd believe me—and we'd gang up on it. Trading myself for Toby would be stupid."

"Sacrifice is very noble." Odett pouted.

"Not if it doesn't accomplish anything," said Amber. "What's to prevent the bogey-monster from accepting Ada for a sacrifice, and then later getting Toby anyway?"

"But then what happened?" wailed Odett, stopping in the middle of the street. "She wouldn't go away and leave us!"

"Of course she wouldn't." Amber, embarrassed, patted her shoulder. "I don't know what happened, and there's no point wondering about it."

178

"But there's nothing else to think about," sniffed Odett. "I'm in that dark room at night, and Ada should be there, and all I can do is wonder where she is—I can't help it!"

Amber fished her handkerchief out of her pocket and wiped Odett's face for her. "Well—I guess if you can't, you can't," she said. "But you'll feel like you wasted a lot of time, when she comes back and tells you all about it."

"Oh, I wish she would! Do you truly think she will?"

"I expect so," Amber said. "But when she does, you're going to be mad as all get-out at her for going away and making you worry. I think"—maybe if Odett took this to heart, Amber'd get some peace—"I think you should work on getting along without her, just to show her. She probably thinks you're falling apart, without her to tag after."

"Mamma said we need to be brave," said Odett. "I don't think I am, though. Ada was. She stood up for women's rights to the teacher and Billy. And you're brave, because you stood up for the deaf boy. And Mamma's brave, because she hasn't let us see her cry." Odett heaved a sigh. "Everybody's brave but me."

"I'm not as brave as you think," said Amber, sincerely. (What did she think the Bauers would do to her if they found out she was Jewish?) "It takes practice. Why don't you stop crying and practice bravery the rest of the way to the store?"

"I haven't been crying," protested Odett, blowing her nose. "I just misted up a little. I'm tip-top now."

Mr. Bauer's store was a yellow-brick building with an RX over the door. Inside a slow fan turned in the ceiling. Simpson manned the soda fountain on the left, and Mr. Bauer, the glass-topped drug counter on the right. "No free ice cream, Ody, sorry," said Simpson. "The boss here is a real Tartar."

"That's not why we came," said Odett, climbing onto a high wrought-iron stool. Glad to turn Odett over to her big brother (who in her opinion did nowhere near his share of work), Amber waited at the pharmacy counter.

The man ahead of her had only one arm, and patches of old, burned skin darkened his face. His baggy, worn-out clothes and shaggy mustache were dirty, and his whole body vibrated slightly. "That last batch was weak," he said, pushing a flat tin box at Mr. Bauer. His voice sounded mushy, as if words were overripe and rotten in his mouth. "I have to take fifteen, twenty-five—They make the stuff weaker every year—"

"The pills were exactly the same strength, Mr. Muller," said Mr. Bauer, gently. "I've explained that to you. The more you take, the more you need. If you would reduce the dosage—"

"I can't!" the man almost screamed. "Don't cheat an old soldier, or—Frieda put you up to it, didn't she? She hates me, that witch, wants to push me into the grave, make her poor old husband suffer because he ain't handsome anymore!"

"Hush, Mr. Muller, you're frightening my daughter!" Odett's eyes were indeed round and scared, and Amber felt her own must be, too. Frieda's husband? "And for sweet Jesus' sake, don't blame your wife!" Mr. Bauer's voice and expression conflicted, as if he wanted to be angry, but was forced to be patient and kind. "If it weren't for Frieda, I'd not supply you at all!"

"They won't do me no good, if you don't give me

enough strength," whined the one-armed man. "I'll go to that River Avenue fellow, and she'll have to come out with the money—"

Mr. Bauer jerked open a drawer and filled the flat box with small grayish tablets. "Very well," he said. "These are the strongest I have. Don't take fifteen, they'd kill you. But do what you please!" He snapped the box shut and thrust it across the counter.

The one-armed man snatched up the box, beginning to eat the tablets before he even got out the door. Mr. Bauer leaned on the counter, breathing hard and shaking. Simpson returned to mixing soda water, and Odett and Amber looked at Mr. Bauer. "Don't tell Frieda about this," he said.

"But Pappa—he didn't pay," protested Odett.

Mr. Bauer made an impatient gesture. "This is a bonus to Frieda's wages she must know nothing about. Promise me!"

Odett crossed her heart. "Honor bright, Pappa."

"What was that you gave him?" asked Amber.

"Opium," said Mr. Bauer.

Amber felt as if he'd hit her in the stomach.

"Mr. Muller's face was scarred and his arm lost in the war, you see," went on Mr. Bauer, in the same calm and rational manner that Dad had used when he first explained to her what a drug addict was. "I remember when Frieda married him. He was bright and handsome, and went into Hood's Texas Brigade alongside my brother. I miss my brother, but when I look at Karl Muller, I'm glad he died instead of coming back like that."

"But why are you giving him opium?" demanded

Amber. Opium, heroin—it was all the same, and she was in a pusher's house!

"It's the soldier's disease," Mr. Bauer explained. "The doctors gave him opium for the pain. And when he returned, the pain continued, and nothing would calm him but more laudanum, opium, morphine—whatever form it could be obtained in. And now the pain is dead, but the craving continues. If he doesn't get it—" Mr. Bauer shrugged. "He has hurt Frieda before now."

"But if you don't give it to him, and he doesn't get any for a while, he can get clean," said Amber. "You can make him quit, cold turkey, and then he won't—" She stopped, reminded of when it was by the way Mr. Bauer looked at her.

"What has turkey to do with anything?" asked Mr. Bauer. "If I don't give him his opium, he will beat the money out of Frieda, or steal it, and buy it at another druggist's." He shrugged. "I can do nothing to protect him from himself—only Frieda from him. I am sorry you had to see that. This is not something fit for children to trouble their heads with." He smiled at her, and made a motion as if clearing the subject away. "What is it you have come for?"

Amber bought the toothache drops, feeling subdued and sick. Drug addicts in 1891! I want to go home! she thought, half hearing Odett's chatter as they walked back to the house. At least there I know what's wrong with the world.

She took the drops straight up to Frieda in her room, which was really a big walk-in closet at the end of the upstairs hall, with one window, a washstand, and a clothes chest. Frieda's face was so swollen she could barely talk, but she smiled miserably in thanks when Amber gave her the medicine. It was unspeakably hot up here. "Would you like me to bring you some ice water?" asked Amber.

Frieda wrinkled up her face and tried to laugh. "Ow!"

"You could wet a washrag in it and cool your face off."

Frieda flapped her fan and nodded, so Amber went to the kitchen, where Mrs. Bauer was chopping onions and Odett was talking about seeing Mr. Muller. "Odett!" snapped Amber. "You promised!"

"I promised not to tell Frieda," said Odett.

Mrs. Bauer shoved her hair off her forehead with the back of her hand and rinsed her knife. "Odett, could you find me a nice big carrot or two?"

Amber got the ice pick and a bowl out of the kitchen cabinet, which was a piece of furniture instead of being built into the wall. The back screen door slammed behind Odett as she ran out to the garden. "Poor Frieda," Amber couldn't help saying. "I wouldn't be her for anything."

"Never let her know that you feel that way," said Mrs. Bauer. "She's a very brave woman and never complains."

"She ought to divorce him."

"What do you know about divorce?" Mrs. Bauer almost gasped.

"What shouldn't I know?" asked Amber in surprise.

"It's these fast times we live in! I was grown-up before I heard that word. What makes you think Frieda can divorce him?"

"I don't know what else she can do." Amber opened the tin-lined oak box that was called a refrigerator, to chip at the block of ice inside. "Mr. Bauer says he hurts her."

"That's not cause for divorce," said Mrs. Bauer. "I don't say it shouldn't be, but it isn't. She has to name another woman."

"Name another woman what?" Amber was no good at chipping ice; all she got were crumbs that melted in the bowl.

Mrs. Bauer sighed. "Do you know what adultery is, in the Ten Commandments?"

Amber was pretty sure she knew, but putting it into terms Mrs. Bauer would know was tricky. "Dating—I mean, walking out with a married person."

"That's right." Mrs. Bauer's face was flushed bright pink. "Those are the only realistic grounds a woman has for divorce." She turned away, laying down her knife. "Never marry, child; it's too big a trap."

At least that was what Amber thought she said, but Mrs. Bauer's back was to her. In a moment Mrs. Bauer walked briskly to the pantry, saying brightly: "Goodness, what a time you're having with the ice! Let me show you how it's done."

By the time Amber took Frieda the ice water and the rag, Doris was up, demanding to be dressed. After that the day went on as usual, ending with reading and sewing on the porch, and prayers which included the usual petition for Ada's safety, sounding more and more mechanical every day. Despite the lack of time to think, Amber figured out when she wrote in her diary that night how she would gain time for herself the next day.

She started her plan by tearing a piece off a roll of cotton batting kept handy for applying calamine lotion, and tucking it under her pillow. The moment she woke up enough next morning to recall her plan, she stuffed it into her mouth, creating a swelling and a slurring of her speech not unlike Frieda's. She kept Mrs. Bauer from looking at the tooth at breakfast by yelling "Ow!" every time Mrs. Bauer came near, and avoided taking the toothache drops by washing them down with a cup of water and spitting the medicine into it. Instead of dressing up to go to church, she was put back to bed, with her face tied up in a towel, as soon as she had Doris and Toby decent.

Fortunately, Frieda was better today and left at her usual time. As soon as Amber was sure she was alone in the house, she whipped off the towel, spat out the cotton, and buttoned her shoes back on. She was safe till evening. After church, the Bauers ate Sunday dinner at Scholz Palm Garden with Mr. Bauer's parents—Oma and Opa, as the kids called them. After Sunday dinner, they would ride the streetcar to Riverside Park, where she would have had even more trouble looking after Doris and Toby than she did at home. Now she had the entire day to herself.

The house seemed huge and quiet, like a house in a dream. Amber danced and sang a Paula Abdul song as she gathered up her diary, a pencil, her purse, and a napkin full of doughnuts. Churchbells echoed distantly, and birds sang nearby. All the people in the neighborhood had gone to church, leaving the houses serene and beautiful. The nineteenth century wouldn't be so bad, Amber thought, if you could get away from people once in a while. She began to fight her way through the sunflowers, humming a song by the New Kids on the Block.

The well breathed cool air into the shadow of the tree above it. Amber sat down with her legs sprawled along the roots and her back to the trunk, unwrapping her doughnuts. "All right, you," she muttered into the well, "I'm going to sit here till I figure you out!"

The well said nothing. Amber spread the napkin on its rim, piled the doughnuts on top, and opened her diary to the first page, where she had tried to arrange what she knew about the well, the wish, and the way it had been granted. That had not come out as much of a list, so she had added another: what she knew about the Haunted Lot. The stories kids told now were pretty much the same as the ones told in the future: lights and movements and stuff. Odett's theory that something had disguised itself as a dog and tried to lure Toby did not fit in with any of that. Whatever haunted the well, it had never been known to do anything in particular, until Amber made her wish.

Amber ate a cinnamon doughnut, thinking. The very first thing she'd heard in this century was Matilda calling for Ada. Could Ada have made a wish in the well, too? Maybe—but if so, what? And why, if it would grant both Ada and Amber their wishes in one afternoon, would it not grant Amber's at night?

Maybe time of day was important. Amber broke off a piece of doughnut. "I wish I lived a hundred years from now," she said, letting it fall.

A small bird landed on the rim of the well opposite her doughnuts and cocked his eye at her. A splashing sounded deep below, and the doughnut piece sailed up again, past the rim of the well, to shatter on the ground. The bird flew to peck up the crumbs. "What? Don't you like doughnuts?" So much for that theory. Amber looked at her notes again and saw that she had used the phrase: "The same day."

That was a brain-twisting idea. She and Ada had not disappeared from their homes on the same day, in any real sense. They had been a hundred years apart, to begin with; and while it had been April 26 when she'd left, it had been April 24 when she'd arrived. But it had been the Friday of Battle of Flowers in both times. Maybe there had to be some sort of connection between days, a bridge across time—but in that case, what exactly would make the bridge, and how could she tell a minute when the bridge existed from a minute when it didn't?

She fed doughnut crumbs to the birds as she tried to make sense of the situation. Where was Ada? How did she fit in? Did she fit in? Amber had the annoying feeling that she had exactly half the information she needed to get back, and that the other half was locked away in some other piece of time.

Or maybe down the well. "Hey, you!" she called, kneeling on the edge. "Give me some help here, will you? What are you? How does this work?"

"Work," echoed the well; and none of the other questions she thought of got any better answers, until she asked, "Where's Ada?"

At that she heard splashing, and something came sailing up out of the well to land, wetly, against the tree roots. Amber jumped back, then bent over the thing. It was a crumpled piece of cloth, gray with water where it was not brown and green with mud and slime. "Ick," she said, pulling on one corner with two fingers. The letters *AB* were embroidered in the corner.

"What you got there?" asked Billy.

Amber almost jumped out of her skin. "Ack! Where'd you come from?"

"My house," said Billy. "I've been practicing moving like an Indian through the deep forest."

"Indians didn't move through deep forest," said Amber. "Not around here."

"I've been reading James Fenimore Cooper's books," said Billy. "Pappa says they're utter nonsense, and he should know, because he's fought Indians. They used to come right into town, during the Comanche moon. But the sneaking through the forest works tip-top, because I just did it. I've been watching you for five minutes."

"Oh, you have not," said Amber, automatically.

"Have too. You were asking the well questions, and when you asked where Ada was, that thing came flying out. So what is it?"

"A handkerchief, I think," said Amber.

Billy reached past her to pick it up. His face changed. "This is Ada's. Pinkie made it for her last year, in thanks for her making new scenery for the puppet theater." He turned on Amber. "How did you get it out of the well?"

Amber folded her arms. "You saw it."

"What I saw didn't make sense." He looked into the well, then at Amber. "Nothing about you makes sense. Amber Burak! What sort of name is that? And where did you learn to bicycle? And how did you get this handkerchief out of the well?"

"That's not what bothers me," said Amber. "What bothers me is, how did it get in there?"

"She can't have fallen in," he said, gazing into the depths.

"What do you care, anyway?" asked Amber. "It's not like she was one of your sisters, or your girlfriend, or anything."

To her surprise, he turned fiery red. "Why shouldn't I care, just as much as if she were my sister? She had—she has a lot more sense than my real sisters do, and if her pappa knew all the dares she's taken, he'd have a fit. I don't think there's anything she couldn't do if she put her mind to it, but you have to push her some." He stopped abruptly, looking at the tree and not at Amber. "Can I have a doughnut?"

"Sure," said Amber, as embarrassed as he was. He must like Ada a lot, to get this het up. She didn't want to have to feel sorry for him, so she stood up to leave. "Take them all. Frieda left some soup on the stove for me."

She marched off through the huisache, along what had been a path before the Haunted Lot became off limits to all the Bauer children. The way Ada must have come, that last day. She went inside and stared at the family picture on the parlor mantel, where everyone, even Toby, looked stiff and prissy. Ada's unfamiliar, stiffly smiling face held no clues.

She must stop worrying about Ada and concentrate on her own problems. She ate thick potato soup (a completely different proposition from the potato soup Mom got out of a can) and then took off her shoes and stockings to lounge on a window seat and work out what she knew. If the date-bridge theory were true, either the day of the week, or the events of that day, must be important. What events were coming up?

It was the fourteenth of June now. The nineteenth was Juneteenth, or Emancipation Day, the anniversary of the day freedom came to the slaves of Texas. That would be a heavy workday for Amber: Mrs. Bauer had invited the Streichers to dinner and Mary Reba, the Streichers' hired girl, had the day off. Amber would probably be tied up looking after kids all afternoon.

Anyway, she wasn't sure anybody would be celebrating Juneteenth in 1991. Her history teacher had said black organizations still arranged picnics and things for June-teenth, but Amber didn't know anybody who went to them. If there was a bridge, from June 19 to June 19, it might not be a big enough one.

The Fourth of July was a better bet. Everybody always celebrated that. She started working up a plan in the diary. She'd have to get away from the kids. Okay. She'd get them playing catch, and deliberately lose the ball in the Haunted Lot, then tell Odett to look after Toby and Doris while she went after it. If the wish didn't work, she'd come right back. If it did . . . she'd leave a note, recommending Ethel for her replacement. Mrs. Bauer had told her Grof was finally going to a deaf school in another town, and Ethel would be at loose ends without him.

Satisfied and tired, Amber put her diary away in her box, and spent the rest of the day reading *St. Nicholas* magazines. If only she had had her tape deck, and a bag of potato chips, and a Coke, the stolen afternoon would have been perfect.

CHAPTER FIFTEEN

Revelations

Mrs. Burak was not pleased with Violet. "I can't help you if you don't trust me," she complained, meeting up with her the next time she went to Streicher.

"You can't help me anyway," Violet said tiredly. "The rules won't let you."

"Perhaps if people followed the rules occasionally, they would work better," Ada suggested. The remark made Mrs. Burak laugh, and nothing more was said on the subject.

Violet had less freedom than Ada, but they managed to get out quite a lot together. Violet was even allowed to sleep over one weekend. Mr. Burak helped them to erect a tent in the backyard. The stars were largely obscured by the lights of the electric city, but right now Venus, Mars, and Jupiter formed a triangle near the crescent moon, so bright they could be seen as clearly as if Old Mr. Burak had hung them from their pecan tree. The girls left the tent flaps open and lay with their heads out.

"Dad said I could tell you," Violet said, linking her

hands behind her head so that her elbows jutted out. "He said if you trusted me, we should trust you."

"You mustn't tell me anything you don't want to," said Ada, virtuously squashing her curiosity.

"I do, though," said Violet, apparently addressing Jupiter. "It's just habit that doesn't want to."

Ada waited, and waited, and finally Violet said, softly: "I hate money."

The remark seemed to call for no response.

"See, people say money doesn't solve everything, but what they don't say is, without money, you can't solve anything!" Violet spoke in a manner unlike her usual one, a few sentences delivered with soft force, followed by a pause, then another few. "There's me, Mom, Dad, and my little sister, Rosesharon. Rosesharon's retarded. Not real bad retarded, not if somebody stays with her, you know? She can do housework, and read a bit. Mom gave up working to stay home and help her."

Ada, who had begun to have an idea how important it was even for women with families to have jobs in these times, said: "It's good that she was able to do that."

"It was all we could do," said Violet firmly. "But Dad got laid off. Then they both looked for work, but nobody found any. And the unemployment ran out. And we had to go for relief, and the rules—the rules wouldn't give us a thing!"

Her voice went so shrill, Ada thought she was crying; but she resumed talking in a more normal tone in a minute. "So—I don't remember how all this worked. I was too young. But for Mom to get enough of the right kind of relief for somebody to stay home with Rosesharon, we couldn't have Dad in the house. So he left. And we told the relief people he abandoned us."

Ada felt her stomach turn over. She stared at the triangle of planets, wondering if the rules really were written as badly as that. She was suddenly glad—she had never thought of it before—that Pappa had his own store.

"So, anyway, that worked for a while. Sometimes he'd come back to see us. Sometimes he got a temporary job and he'd have cash for us. But Rosesharon's older now, and I'm older, and Grandma broke her hip and came to live with us, and everything's more expensive, and the social worker started talking about special schools for retarded kids. Special programs. And she said the best way to get Rosesharon educated would be to give up our right to her. Give her to the courts."

"But—what for?" asked Ada.

Violet shrugged and sighed. "I don't understand it all, and I don't think the social worker did, either. But I'll tell you what. Mom joined this group for the parents of retarded kids, and this woman in it, she let the court have her son—and when she had him, he could walk and dress himself and talk just fine. And the last time she saw him, he was sitting in a corner, and he couldn't say his own name, and he'd forgot how to walk."

A bubble of disbelief swelled in Ada. It couldn't be this bad! God would not let things truly be that bad!

"So we won't give Rosesharon to the courts. To the court she's just another retarded kid, but to us . . ." Violet stopped again, and was quiet for a long time.

"So you ran away, like your father did," Ada said, "so your mother didn't have so many expenses."

"That's right," said Violet. "I can take care of myself, and Dad and me, we keep track of each other. While I was gone, we saw Mom and Rosesharon and Grandma in a park a couple times. Rosesharon's doing fine. Grandma taught her to knit, and she's making me a sweater." Violet took her hands out from behind her head, and sat up on her elbows. "I think it's going to be kind of lumpy," she said, half laughing.

Ada rolled over onto her stomach, propping herself on her elbows, too. She felt awkward, lying so close to Violet, hearing such confidences, and not touching her. "It's hard to believe," she said, her eyes on the triangle of planets, "that God lets such things happen."

"God's let worse things than that happen," said Violet. "Slavery, and concentration camps, and—and—"

"Indian massacres," said Ada. "And the War Between the States, and—oh, I want to go home!"

"Me, too," sighed Violet, laying down her head.

Ada felt a bit odd about entering the upper story of the Streicher Children's Center. What would Mrs. Streicher think, if she could see her house overrun by children of every size, race, and disposition, her waxed floors covered with cheap carpet, her spacious rooms divided into dormitories? Yet there was nothing to be accomplished in the Haunted Lot, and it was so hot outdoors that Ada eventually succumbed to Violet's urging that they go into the air-conditioned Center.

"I've even got a room to myself," Violet bragged, leading her upstairs. "It's almost a closet, except it has a window, but they needed beds so bad—what's the matter?"

"I'm utterly staggered! You've got Billy's room!"

Ada had told Violet about Billy, and how his family thought he hung the moon in the sky. "Why'd they stick him in a closet?" Violet asked. "I thought his folks treated him like Mr. Big."

"There wasn't any other place to put him," said Ada. "Not unless they crowded three of his sisters into one room. It wasn't a closet, it was the hired girl's room; only Mary Reba went home every night." She laid her hand on the doorknob at the end of the hall. "This one, right?"

"Right," said Violet.

Ada swung open the door and stepped in. Billy would have been upset. The shelves for his treasured botanical and geological samples (referred to by Mary Reba as his "trashy weeds and rocks") were stacked with Violet's magazines and personal toiletries. The space underneath had been enclosed for a cupboard, and the walls, for which Billy had carefully chosen a horse-motif paper, were covered with white plasterboard. Violet's bed replaced his black-painted iron bedstead under the window, where there were white venetian blinds instead of the paper screen his oldest sister, Jane, had painted for him.

Ada knelt on the bed and pulled the cord to open the blinds. Playground, parking lot, Haunted Lot (the well a mere shadow), blue warehouse. "You see where that water pipe is on the warehouse?" She pointed. "That was about where Odett's and my window was. We used to signal back and forth to Dot and Pinkie with a candle. Billy would pretend to be them to tease us, so we had to pay attention to just where the light came from. He could see into our room, if we forgot to pull the blind."

"He spied on you? What a creep!"

Ada shrugged. "I don't think he would have been so bad if he'd had even one brother. But he had six sisters, and both his brothers died before they were three, so everybody spoiled him." She couldn't help smiling smugly. "Everybody but me." She turned her back on the saddening view, so nearly familiar, and kicked off her canvas shoes to put her feet up on the bed. "He'd have a fit if he saw his room now. I wonder how this house ever got turned into a children's center."

Violet shrugged. "Once the highway went through, nobody'd want to live here regular. I expect his kids sold out."

"But then they wouldn't have called it the Streicher Center," Ada pointed out. "Somebody in the family must have donated it."

"There's a picture of some people in the dining room," said Violet. "I never looked at it."

"Billy used to threaten us with mutilation and death if we came in here, and Mary Reba wasn't allowed to move anything when she dusted." She stuck her head over the bed and examined the carpet. "I wonder if the workmen who remodeled this room found his secret hiding place here by the window?"

"How do you know where his secret hiding place was?" asked Violet, sitting on the floor with her back against the cupboard.

"He stole my best gloves one time, and while he was out I came in and hunted till I found them." The thin, colorless carpet was raggedly cut to fit the floor, and did not seem to be fastened down. Ada calculated the location of the loose board, and ran her fingers along the gap between the plasterboard and the floor. She felt the board give. "Here it is," she said, pushing down and watching the shape of the carpet change. "Help me move the bed, and I'll show you."

Violet helped gladly, and they soon had the bed pushed almost to the door and the carpet turned up. The loose board had begun to rot, and crumbled slightly as Ada raised it, exposing the space between the floor of the second story and the ceiling of the first. The light from the window didn't reach far enough, so the musty-smelling hole was impenetrably dark.

"Ick," said Violet. "What if there's mice?"

"Mice don't bite much," said Ada. She plunged in her arm to the elbow, feeling about on the gritty floor until she touched a metallic edge. "Eureka!"

"Your what?" Violet crowded her, trying to see in.

"Eureka," said Ada impatiently, grasping the object and drawing it out. "It means 'I've found it.' Billy's secret box!" She blew off the dust. "Have you got anything to pry with? The lid's stuck."

Violet fetched a comb with metal teeth, narrow enough to pry with, and they soon had the box open. Inside lay a crumpled, dirty square of cloth, and a copybook. "That's my handkerchief!" exclaimed Ada indignantly. "The one Pinkie embroidered my initials on!"

"You didn't take very good care of it," remarked Violet, lifting out the copybook.

"It's the one I was carrying the day I made the wish, and when I arrived here I didn't have it." Ada tried to smooth it, but all she did was create numerous small tears

197

at the creases. It had been badly soiled, and left crumpled like this—she shivered—for a hundred years.

"Matilda was good at chemistry," commented Violet, turning pages that smelled of old ink and old paper.

"Yes," said Ada, proudly. "But what would Billy want with her copybook?"

"To cheat in chemistry with?" suggested Violet.

The neat ink entries gave way to a sprawling hand in lead pencil. "That's not Matilda's writing. What's it say?"

Violet squinted and read. " 'Point one. Something lives in the Haunted Lot, probably down the well, probably intelligent.' "

"What?" Ada rudely snatched away the book, and Violet let her. Ada skimmed the page, then the next. With a trembling hand she pointed to the bottom of the third page: " 'Ada disappeared from 1891, and I disappeared from 1991. We're about the same age, look sort of alike, and have the same initials. I wonder if that means anything? Sometimes I think it has to, and sometimes I think it can't.' "

"Oh," said Violet. "Oh!" She jerked open the drawer of the tiny bureau, scattering underthings till she found Amber's hair ribbon and flung it down next to the handkerchief. "It's her, isn't it? It's Amber!"

"It must be," agreed Ada, still skimming. "See, here's Dr. Cunningham, and the Streicher Center—and—goodness—"

"What's the matter?"

Ada almost edited the paragraph, but Violet would read it for herself soon, and anyway it was too late to have secrets. She read aloud: " 'If Mom and Dad staying together means they wind up like the Bauers, I guess I don't mind him going to Austin so much. I wish I could get home and tell them whatever they want is fine. I wish I could get home at all.' "

"It's got to be Amber," said Violet. Her eyes shone and she began to talk faster. "I bet the thing in the well can't switch you unless you're in the same place at the same time. I mean—not the same time, but—what would be the same times, if—you know what I mean."

Ada reviewed her vocabulary lessons and found the right word. "Analogous times," she said, "but what's the important factor? The Battle of Flowers? Or Friday? It wasn't the date, because that was different."

"Turn to the end," urged Violet. "See how it came out."

Obediently Ada turned over several pages until she came to a blank, when she turned back. Half a page of pencil scrawl ended with another abrupt change of hand-writing—Billy's hand, in bold ink strokes, saying:"Hi Ada you snoop!"

"Well, forevermore," said Ada.

"Never mind that dude," said Violet. "What does Amber say?"

" 'I'll give the Fourth of July a shot. I can get away from the kids long enough to throw my fireball in the well. People are talking about parades and balls and it looks like we'll be out all day, so I'd better do it as early as I can. If the Fourth doesn't work, I don't know what I'll do. I wish that thing in the well would talk!' "

"The Fourth of July," said Violet. "Honey, we've got to get you to that well the morning of the Fourth!"

Time crawled.

The Buraks all noticed that Ada was nervous, but she

resisted their attempts to find out why, and they respected her silence. The switch would work; it had to work—but what would happen to the Buraks when the child they had bent the rules for vanished? And how could she just go off and leave Violet?

Violet, however, did not appear to feel that she would be deserted. "Hey, I'd be bugging out on you soon anyway," she pointed out. "To keep ahead of the Man. You couldn't do me any good, and even if you could, your family's more important."

"That's true," Ada admitted, "but I'll never forget you."

"I heard that!" Violet laughed. "Tell you what, make a million dollars and leave it to me in your will, okay? My real last name's Little. Remember that!"

On the third of July, Mr. Burak and Old Mr. Burak took Ada and Violet to see *The Rocketeer*, a movie that showed a real man—not a cartoon—apparently really flying. Though she had seen flying on TV, Ada was astonished at the difference a wall-sized screen made and found herself laughing and clapping her hands, or crying out and covering her eyes, even at places where no one else in the audience reacted.

"Anybody'd think you never saw a movie before," remarked Mr. Burak.

"Oh, but it was wonderful," Ada defended herself. "Cartoons are the best, though."

"We do know it's wonderful," said Old Mr. Burak. "The original cels—the drawings—from those Disney movies get displayed in art museums, they're so good. But kids today all grew up with animation and special effects. You don't expect anybody over five to pop her eyes out of her head and squeal at stuff on a movie screen, even when it looks like a real guy really flying."

"*One Hundred and One Dalmatians* starts tomorrow," said Mr. Burak. "We can all go, and Ada can remind us how good it is."

Ada said nothing.

The morning of the Fourth, Ada woke with a nervous ache in her stomach. She dressed in the green dress and buttoned shoes that were all that remained of her original clothes, blushing at the thought of what her mother and sisters would say when they saw her stockings and underthings. At breakfast she got permission to go to the Streicher Center to be with Violet while the Buraks gathered up other children from various centers for the arranged outing.

"I've got something for Violet," Mr. Burak said, "so don't be late. Meet you on the front porch at eleven-thirty."

"Yes, sir," Ada said, looking from him to Mrs. Burak. "I'm truly grateful for all you've done for me."

Mrs. Burak laughed and kissed her. "You don't have to keep telling us that, Ada. We like having you."

Violet met her at the Center gate, and she delivered Mr. Burak's message as they headed down the street, pretending not to be going to the Haunted Lot. "What could he have for me?" asked Violet. "And why not deliver it at the movie last night?"

"Could it be anything to do with your family?"

"I can't think what." Violet frowned. "Anyway, don't you worry about it. Us Littles can take care of each other."

The huisache was mostly done blooming, but the sun-

flowers made up for it. Green-backed, white-bellied locusts gossiped in thick clusters on the roots of the stump,
and a horned toad slipped into the shadow of a rock. Ada
drew three chocolate bars out of her pocket. "I wish we
knew exactly when Amber's going to wish," she said,
handing one to Violet and peeling the paper off another.
The third sat on the well rim between them as they ate.

"It's bound to work," declared Violet. "Otherwise why
would the diary stop there? Why would Billy leave you
that note?"

Ada savored her candy. Most twentieth-century food
was dreadful, but she had no complaint about chocolate
bars. Wiping her hands on a piece of tissue, she drew out
her purse and removed the modern money. "Here," she
said, holding it out, "I can't use this where I'm going."

"I'll give it back to the Buraks for you." Violet licked her
fingers and folded the money into the pocket of her shorts.

"I'd rather you kept it," said Ada.

Violet shook her head. "That'd be stealing."

"It would not. It was my money, and I gave it to you."

"It's the state's money that the Buraks got to take care
of you and they passed it on."

"You don't mind when the state's money feeds you and
puts you in shelters," Ada pointed out.

"But it'd cost the state more to take care of Rosesharon
than it does to take care of me." She grinned, and Ada
could not tell whether she was serious. "I'm doing the
state a favor."

Ada gave up. Violet would be what she was, whatever
anyone said to her. She looked into the well, and picked
up the last candy bar. "I suppose I may as well try it now,"
she said.

"Good luck," said Violet.

Ada unwrapped the bar. "When I come from, best friends say good-bye by kissing and hugging each other."

Violet made a face. "When you come from is pretty mushy, but all right. If you'll feel better." She was plainly not used to being hugged, staying stiff; but Ada kissed her just as she soon hoped to kiss Odett and Matilda. "Now watch," said Violet. "Now we're all set, it won't work."

Ada shrugged, dropped the candy bar into the well, and leaned over the darkness. "I wish to go home, please!" she called, low and clear; and low and clear, the splash and the echo came back at her, as the world began to spin.

Firecrackers popped.

Shade fell across her shoulders.

Toby cried: "Ada!"

Billy added: "Great Caesar's ghost!"

Ada scooped up her little brother and whirled him in the air with a happy cry, dirty though he was.

CHAPTER SIXTEEN

Turn and Return

Amber's diary disappeared on Juneteenth.

She knew what had happened to it. After lunch, Billy had gone upstairs with Simpson to look at the older boy's rock collection, and he'd come down by himself. It must have been easy to slip into the nursery and check out the box at the foot of Amber's bed.

Billy acted as if nothing had happened, and she decided (after some gritting of teeth and cussing) that the best thing she could do was act the same. If she made a fuss, he would realize that the diary's contents were important, but if she ignored it, he wouldn't know what to think. She hoped.

The morning of the Fourth, Toby and Doris rousted her out of bed while the sky was still dim. Amber had convinced Mrs. Bauer that Toby's long hair and skirts increased his chances of being burned by a stray spark, and he was going into his first pair of pants this very day. In honor of his new grown-up status he was especially well behaved for almost ten minutes, at which time Matilda spoiled it by mentioning the parade.

This reminded him of his last parade, when he had been nearly run over, and nothing less than Mrs. Bauer's personal attention could calm his fears. The others also looked subdued. "Such a lot has changed since the last parade," said Matilda, poking at her scrambled eggs.

"Maybe Ada will come back," suggested Odett, hopefully.

Mrs. Bauer rocked Toby back and forth. The family looked at their full plates. "What about those fireworks?" Amber asked Simpson, to break the silence.

"I want to set some off this year!" said Odett at once.

"Me, too," said Doris. "I'm almost six now."

"Six isn't big enough," said Mr. Bauer. "Odett may light sparklers. But don't use them up! You don't want to be the only ones without them at the park."

"But we can set off some?" Odett looked so pleading Simpson laughed.

"Sure. May we be excused, sir?"

Mr. Bauer having nodded permission, Matilda, Odett, Doris, and Simpson all wiped their mouths and rose. Seeing them headed for the door, Toby forgot that he had been upset. "I go with you," he cried.

Amber had to take whatever chance she could get. "I forgot my handkerchief," she said to Matilda. "I'll come in a minute."

She hurried upstairs to make sure she had everything and to write a note.

"Dear Mr. and Mrs. Bauer and all, I'm sorry to run out on you, but I must try to return to my own family. You have all been real good to me, and I hope Ada comes back. I think

Ethel Schneider could look after Doris and Toby better than I can, anyway. Here's what's left of the money you gave me. I won't need it where I hope to go. Thanks so much for everything.''

That looked completely inadequate; but what would be adequate? She signed her name and slipped down the front stairs, tiptoed through the parlor to the side door. Mrs. Bauer and Frieda were rattling plates in the kitchen. Amber slipped out.

Ducking past the windows, glancing toward the street where Simpson was lighting a string of firecrackers for the children, Amber ran to the Haunted Lot. The air smelled of dust, roses, and the smoldering punk sticks with which the children lit their fireworks. Dogs barked. Firecrackers hissed and banged. Amber ran to the well and reached into her pocket for her fireball.

"Amber! A-amber! Wait up!"

Amber stamped her foot in disgust. Toby's cap hung askew, his long hair straggled around his anxious face, and his brand-new pants were already dirty. He ran up to her and grabbed her leg. "Don't go, don't go!" he cried. "Can't go in the lot! You'll go like Ada!"

"Oh, Toby," moaned Amber. "Now you've spoiled it!"

Toby shook his head and held on as tight as he could, both arms wrapped around her knee and his face pressed into her skirt. "Don't go, don't go!" he repeated, so upset that Amber hadn't the heart to be mad at him. She sat down on the edge of the well and hugged him, considering what to do.

She couldn't make the wish with him here. If it worked,

and she vanished, he'd be all alone with the well, and might decide to go looking for her in it. Yet, if she took him back to the others, she was likely to lose her chance.

Amber was still dithering when Billy arrived, crashing carelessly through sunflowers and whistling. "Why, hello, Amber!" he said, in fake surprise. "What the dickens are you doing here?"

Toby appealed to Billy. "Don't let her go, don't let her go!" he entreated. "She'll go like Ada!"

"You know why I'm here," said Amber, though not as coldly as she might have. "You read about it in that copybook you stole."

"Me? Steal? Ma'am, you cut me to the quick!"

"Yeah, well, now you're here you can make yourself useful." Amber bent over Toby. "You be good and mind what Billy says, okay? And don't be scared. I'm going home."

"Home?" repeated Toby doubtfully.

Billy's face changed. "You really mean to do it, then? Make a wish in a well and hope some fairy or other sends you—"

"To 1991, that's right," said Amber. "And you can think I'm crazy if you want. If this works it won't matter, and if it doesn't"—her stomach hurt something awful—"I'll have to live with it. Just make sure if I vanish Toby doesn't go jumping into the well after me, okay?"

"You're the strangest girl I ever met," said Billy.

Amber ignored him and spoke to Toby. "You be brave now. I know you're brave, or you wouldn't have come to save me. Nothing's going to hurt me, and if you hang on tight to Billy, nothing can hurt you, either." She pulled the atomic fireball out of her pocket and bent over the well. "Here goes nothing."

"Great Caesar's ghost, Amber, this is crazy!"

Amber shrugged, dropped the fireball into the well, and leaned over the darkness. "I wish to go home, please!" she called, low and clear; and low and clear, the splash and the echo came back at her, as the world began to spin.

Firecrackers popped.

The smell of roses and dust gave way to the smell of gasoline fumes and sun-hot rock.

The light of the sun, the sound of locusts and highway, the weight of the air, dropped on her as suddenly as a blanket dropped onto her head. She started sweating at once.

"Excellent!" said a half-familiar voice.

Amber turned, and saw a girl she thought she ought to know. One of Mom's placements? "Um," she said.

"S'cool," said the girl. "I'm Violet. A friend of Ada's."

"Ada? Then she—you mean Ada Bauer, right?"

"Uh-huh. Y'all switched places." Violet grinned, but blinked her eyes rapidly. "We found your diary and figured it out that you and her had to be in about the same place at about the same time for old what's-its-face in the well to switch you back. So we guessed when you'd be able to get here, and it worked." Violet nevertheless looked a little brought down.

Amber, finding her legs shaking, sat down on the edge of the well. "So Ada's back home, too? Daisy!"

"It'll be a real rip if she's not, but I guess we'll never know for sure."

A giggle echoed from the depths of the well, and both Violet and Amber leaned over, to see if they could catch sight of anything; but it was no go. "I'm about fed up with that critter," said Violet.

"It's not its fault Ada and I made stupid wishes," said Amber. "Where're my folks?"

"They're supposed to be here at eleven-thirty to take some kids for a picnic, but I don't think we should make them wait so long," said Violet. "They're totally bummed about you."

Amber stood up, her legs feeling more solid. "I'll call them right now!"

Her sudden appearance in the Streicher Center caused consternation among the staff, but she ignored it and went straight to the phone. When no one answered at her house, she called Grandad, who almost had a heart attack. When she got him to let her go she called all the centers Mom and Dad were picking up kids at. That done, she went to sit on the porch with Violet and get caught up on current events.

At least Mom and Dad hadn't gotten divorced while she was gone. They would probably do it now, though. It was a depressing prospect, and she put off thinking about it. She heard all about Ada's rescue from the mental hospital with strong interest. "You think they'll feel like they have to put me away if I tell them the truth?" she asked.

Violet shrugged. "I don't know. They already heard Ada's story, and I'll back you up—and your diary's up-stairs."

"I think I'll risk it," said Amber. "I had to tell a lot of lies, back in 1891, and I'm sick of it. And I don't have a story made up, anyway."

Mom and Dad arrived before ten, having left the chil-dren with someone else. Amber ran out to the car, and for a minute thought she was going to smother, they hugged her so tight. Grandad arrived before anyone had a chance to complete a sentence, and she was hugged some more, while Mom cried and Dad kept touching her as if to make sure she was still fastened together right. By the time they returned to the porch, Violet was gone.

"But where have you been?" asked Dad, trying to sound stern and not succeeding. "We thought you were dead!"

"And where did you get those clothes?" asked Mom.

Amber looked down at her button boots, white stockings, full blue skirt, and button-down-the-back blouse. "This'll be hard for you to believe," she said, "but you know what Ada Bauer told you? About being from 1891? It was true. We switched places."

Mom groaned. Dad sighed. "Okay, let's hear your version."

So Amber told them, plowing ahead even after she realized that they were not buying any of it. Grandad stopped looking at her, watching the sky instead; except when she told him she wanted to start going to synagogue with him on Saturdays. Dad looked sterner and sterner, and Mom put her face into her hands. "I know it's weird," Amber finished. "But that's the way it happened. Violet says she's got my diary. And Ada's gone."

"Why are you doing this to us, Amber?" asked Dad in a hopeless voice. "Is it because Dr. Cunningham told you we were getting divorced?"

"No," said Amber. "And—and it's—it's okay with me if you split up. I mean, I won't like it, but—just don't make me decide who I want to live with right away, okay?"

"We're not getting divorced if we can help it," said Mom into her hands. "When your dad got that chance at the

Austin job, and me for that promotion, neither of us was willing to give up those chances to stay together. It looked like we loved our jobs more than each other, and if that's so, we shouldn't be married. But we're only separated right now."

"And we're running up a heck of a phone bill," said Dad. "I keep coming home to this empty apartment and wanting to tell your mom about what happened that day. Not to mention wanting you. The more I think about it, the less I think we should make this permanent." He looked at Amber gravely. "So does that change any part of your story?"

Amber shook her head. "No, sir," she whispered.

The sound of the highway emphasized the absence of speech.

"So Ada's gone now?" asked Grandad after a while. "And that Violet kid will back up your story?"

Amber nodded.

Mom was crying. "I can't believe you children would do this to me!" she said. "I knew Vi was a bit of a con, but I never thought Ada and you would—would—"

"We didn't!" Amber huddled against her mother. "I don't know Violet, and I never saw Ada, and I wish I could prove it!"

"I guess we'd better go upstairs and have a talk with Vi," said Dad. "Assuming she hasn't slipped out the back way! I have a little duty to discharge regarding her, anyway."

Dad fetched a large metal box from the backseat, and they went in, brushing off the attention of the staff. Violet's room was much like Frieda's. When Violet let them in, there was barely space for everyone. With red eyes and

211

straight back, she gave a handful of money to Mom. "Here's what's left of Ada's allowance," she said. "I'm going to be totally up front with you, whatever you want to ask me, unless it might get my own folks in a mess."

Dad put the box down and picked up a small box sitting open on the bed. "Are these your evidences of time travel?"

"That's right," said Violet. "We found the handkerchief and the diary in Billy Streicher's secret hiding place. The thing in the well threw Amber's hair ribbon at us. It is yours, right?" she asked, pointing.

"That's right," said Amber, recognizing all three items in the box. "And that's Matilda's copybook I kept my diary in, and the handkerchief the thing in the well threw at me."

"You've obviously planned this well," said Mom, her voice brittle as old paper. "Why don't we try getting at some basic facts? Like what your real name is, Vi."

"Violet Angela Little," said Violet, folding her arms.

They all stared at one another, nobody sure what to say next. Grandad broke the silence. "What's in this box?" he asked, laying his hand on the one Dad had brought up from the car.

Dad made a face. "Another mystery. It was entrusted to my new firm in Austin thirty years ago, with instructions that it was to be opened July 1, 1991. So they did that, and the instructions direct me—by name—to take this box to Violet Little, a child known to me, residing at the Streicher Children's Center, and present it to her on July 4. And sure enough, the only Violet I know is claiming the name Little, but . . ." His eyebrows drew together, and he shook his head.

Violet's face changed.

"Who wrote the instructions?" asked Grandad.

"That's even weirder. Mrs. William Streicher, the old woman who set up this shelter."

Violet made a small sound in her throat. Amber saw that they were both thinking the same thing.

"What are we standing around for, then?" asked Mom impatiently. "This at least is something we can get to the bottom of. Let's open the box!"

"The instructions are for Vi to do that." Dad handed a key to Violet. She had to turn it with both hands, the lock was so stiff, but the lid went up easily, releasing an antique smell. Inside were stacks of albums, like the ones Grandad kept his stamps and coins in, and manila envelopes. On top lay a yellow-and-white envelope addressed: "To Violet, Love Ada."

Violet touched the name with a gentle forefinger. "Ada," she said. "Mrs. Billy Streicher."

"How could she marry Billy?" demanded Amber. "He was a total jerk!"

Violet handed the envelope to Dad. "Here. I don't want nobody saying I pulled any switches."

Grandad laid the manila envelopes aside to get at the albums as Dad began to read.

February 20, 1961

My dear Violet,

If all has gone well, you will read this within a few hours of my disappearance, and Amber's reappearance. Since the moment I returned to 1891, to find both Bill and Toby astonished at Amber's going and my return, I have rested easy in the conviction that the experiment was a complete success. If something did go awry, please express my condolences to Mr. and Mrs. Burak, whose great kindness to me I have always remembered, just as I have always remembered yours.

Bill was the last person I would have chosen to share my secret, but he proved helpful in convincing my family not to question me too nearly about the details of my adventure, and in making the incident fade into something normal in Toby's young mind. Poor Toby was very frightened at first, but by now he is certain that he remembers Amber running away, and my returning, in a conventional manner. I wish I could have met Amber. She made a vast impression on my family in the short time she was here—especially her bicycle feats and her championing of the deaf boy at the orphanage. We had his big sister, Ethel, for a hired girl for several years, and she never tired of telling how her brother, Grof, was saved from the home for the feebleminded—or the retarded, as I'm supposed to call them now.

There is so much I would tell you! But this pen is heavy, and I am old—eighty-three in August, can you believe?—and you will not be born before I am laid to rest.

The items in this box are all for you. It has troubled me since my return that, after all you did for me, I could do nothing for your benefit; and might even have done you harm, for if Mr. and Mrs. Burak inquire into my disappearance, might not you and Amber both be subject to any number of suspicions?

Mom and Dad looked at each other. "I don't believe it," said Dad. "But this was in the vault for thirty years. It had dust like fur on it, and mouse tracks in the dust."

Grandad laid aside a stamp album and picked up an album of coins. Violet stood by the window, looking toward the Haunted Lot. Amber hugged herself, clenching and unclenching her jaws.

"I don't believe it, either," said Mom. "But keep reading."

Therefore, Bill and I became avid collectors of stamps and coins. Every new American issue from that time to this, with the exception of gold coins (now illegal to own) and with the addition of some older issues, is included here in the best condition we could obtain. After taking precautions to ensure the legality of the proceedings I have in mind, I entrust this box and certain papers to the Austin firm for which Mr. Burak will someday work, directed specifically to him. I trust this will be convincing proof of the truths you and Amber should tell. I also trust I have selected the right firm! The business card Mrs. Burak kept with the emergency numbers had a note with their name on it. But I am almost certain I recall the first partners.

I trust, as well, that the contents of this box will be of help to your family in its troubles. Old Mr. Burak will be able to tell you roughly how well I have succeeded in doing for you. Everything in this box is yours, free and clear and absolute.

Everybody looked at Grandad. "It's quite a collection," he said. "I don't know how much money Vi thinks she needs, but if there really is every issue of every American stamp and coin since 1891 in these albums, it's got to add up to a tidy sum."

"Enough to live on for a year, or what?" demanded Violet.

Grandad shrugged. "A lot depends on the state of the market. Does that letter say what's in the envelopes?"

Dad started reading again.

In addition, I have included a smaller collection of my own. Remembering something Old Mr. Burak said about animation cels appearing in art museums, I took some pains, when animated cartoons began appearing, to obtain examples of my favorites. Do you remember Mr. Burak offering to take us to 101 Dalmatians? I regretted then that I would never see it, but last night I did! I will get hold of a cel if I can, preferably of Sgt. Tibs shielding all those pups with his body. I doubt these will ever be worth much financially, but at least you will have something to remember me by, as I have always remembered you. My Bill is dead, and though I have mourned the changes of the times less than most old folks I know, I am tired. Now that I have seen Dalmatians *and done the best I could to return the many favors of my dear friend, I feel that I can die satisfied.*

With fondest regards to the Buraks, I remain,

Yours for all time,

Ada Bauer Streicher.

Violet's silent head was dark against the white square of the window. Grandad was already opening the envelopes, producing tissue-wrapped cels, clean and sharp and brightly colored. Snow White dancing for the dwarfs,

Dumbo clutching his "magic" feather, Sleeping Beauty in her peasant dress, Pinocchio with his nose sprouting leaves. Grandad whistled softly. "I don't know much about the market, but I'm sure a normal family could live for a year off any one of these. If these really are incontestably yours—"

"She wouldn't have said that if they weren't," said Violet in a high, quavering voice. She whirled around and squirmed through the crowd of bodies, looking up at Mom and blinking. "You believe her, don't you? Amber and I are telling the truth, and all that stuff in the box is mine."

"I don't understand it," said Mom slowly, "but I've been trying and trying, and I can't find a way not to believe it."

"Then I got to call my dad," said Violet. "He won't believe it, either, but—I got to call my dad!" She shoved her way out and thundered down the hall.

Grandad put the cels back into the envelope carefully. "Isn't there some picture of the founder downstairs?" he asked.

"I don't know what difference you think that'll make," said Dad, but when they finished putting everything back into the box and locking it, they trooped down to the dining room. The staff was cooking hot dogs. Violet was talking on the office phone.

The portrait hung over the fireplace, a middle-aged woman with round glasses and brown hair, and a man standing behind her. The woman meant nothing to Amber, but she saw in the man's face an echo of the boy who had lived here, a few hours and a hundred years ago.

Mom, Dad, and Grandad had eyes only for the woman.

"I never noticed this before. It does look like her," said Mom, "that polite smile that shuts you out completely."

"Somebody'll have to take a look at that well," said Grandad.

"It won't do you any good," said Violet, coming in. "That critter's the most uncooperative thing you ever almost saw." She stood next to Amber. "My dad's on his way. He thinks I've flipped out. Somebody'll have to drag him upstairs before he grabs me and runs off." She looked at Grandad. "You'd better do it, because he trusts lawyers and social workers about as far as he can throw the Alamo, and it's going to be pretty bogus if we can't convince him. Okay?"

"Okay," said Grandad. "I'll do my best."

"Ada'll convince him tip-top," said Amber. "And then can we take him and Violet for pizza? I haven't had any in a hundred years."